STAR WARS™

THE PHANTOM MENACE

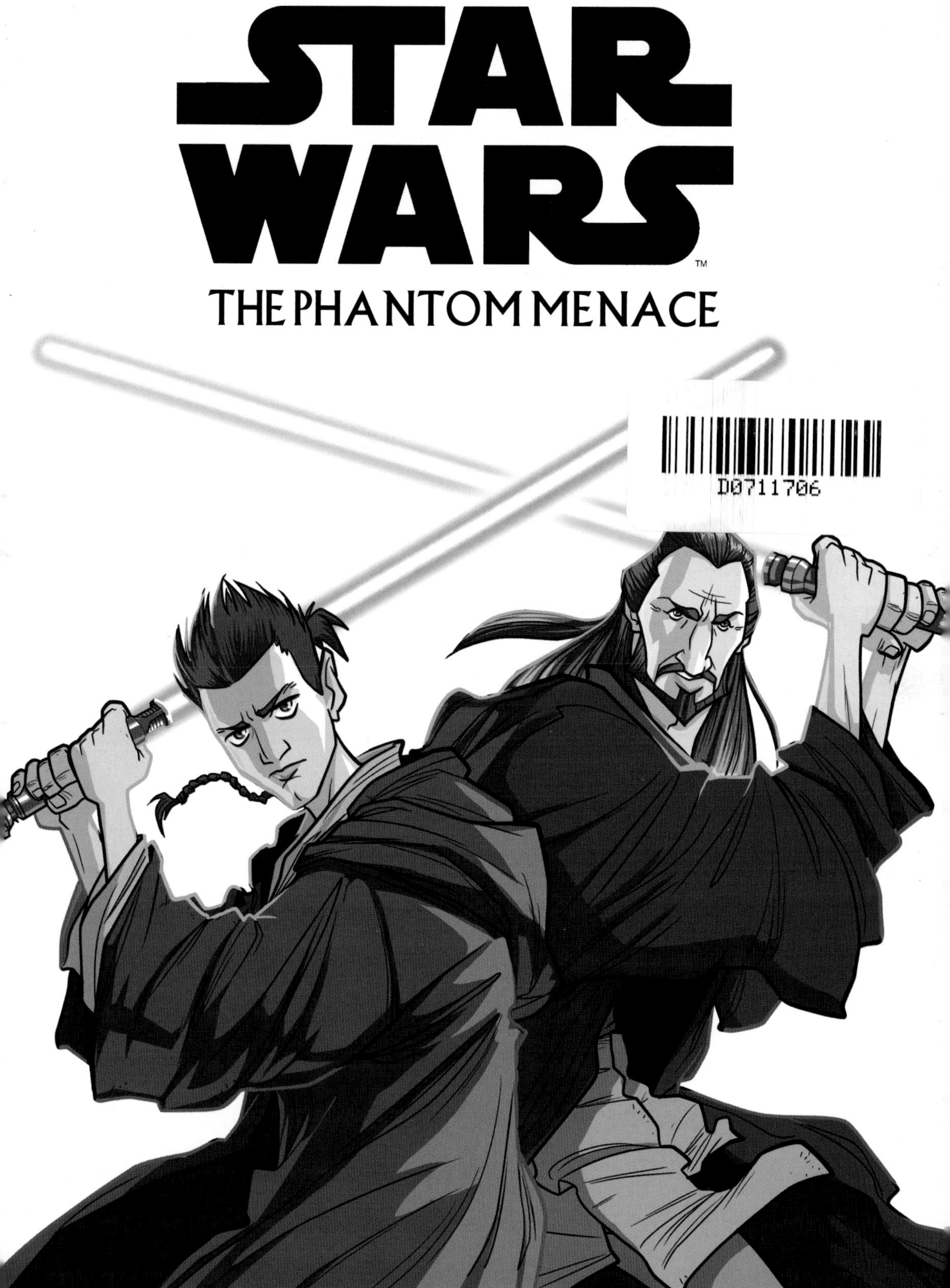

A LONG TIME AGO, IN A GALAXY FAR, FAR AWAY...

Meet the CHARACTERS

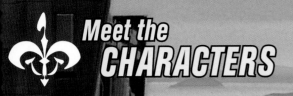

QUI-GON JINN

Experienced **warrior** and **wise Jedi Master**, Qui-Gon Jinn is always ready to take great risks for what he believes is right – even if that means disagreeing with the **Jedi High Council**. When he first encounters Anakin Skywalker, Qui-Gon clearly feels that Anakin has some part to play in the future of the galaxy.

OBI-WAN KENOBI

Loyal and often more cautious than his master, Obi-Wan Kenobi is Jinn's **Padawan**. He does his best to be worthy of the **Jedi Order**, but even if he does not always agree with Qui-Gon's choices he follows his example.

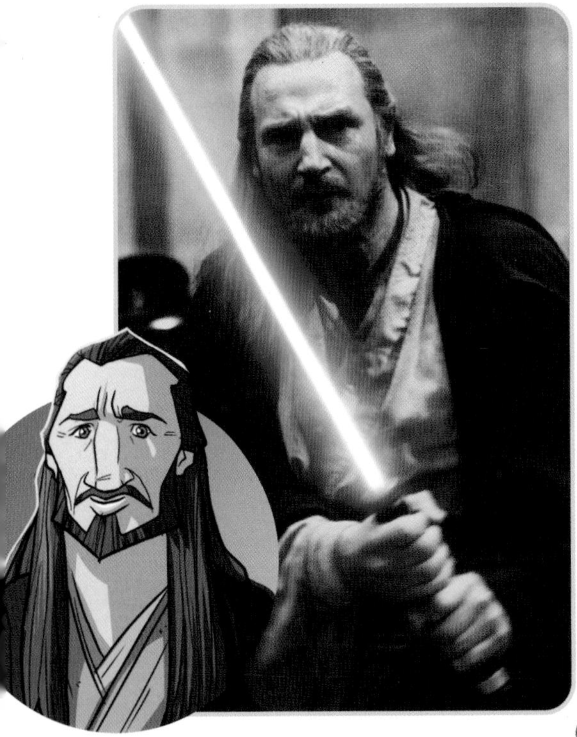

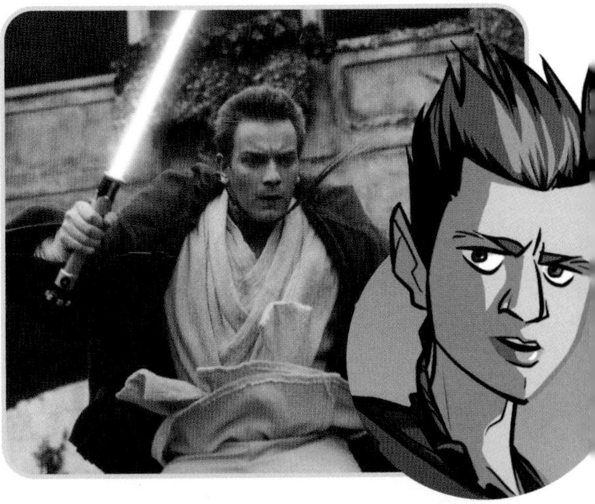

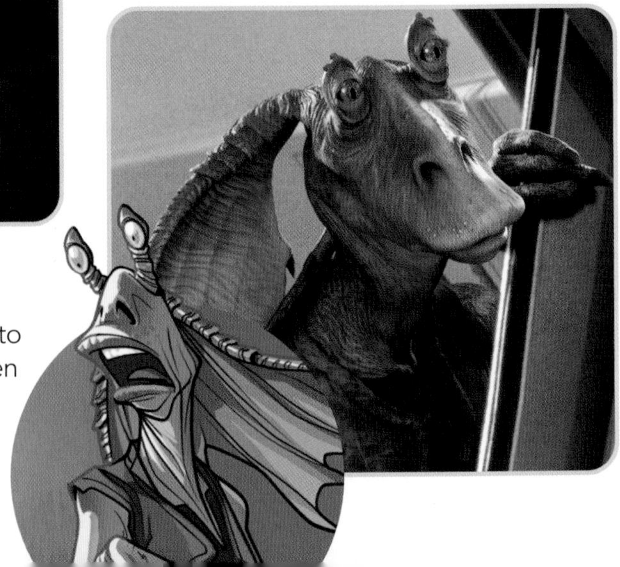

JAR JAR BINKS

Like all **Gungans**, Jar Jar is native to the **planet Naboo**, but he has been exiled from his home city because of his clumsiness – which caused all sorts of trouble in the past.

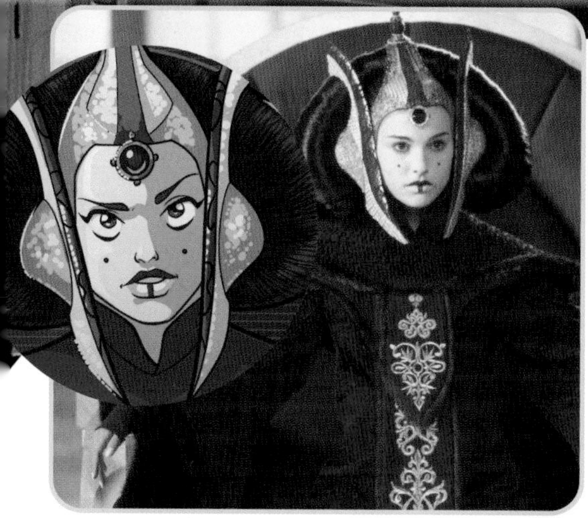

QUEEN AMIDALA

Despite her young age, Padmé Amidala is a **determined** and **sensible ruler**. Elected by the people of Naboo when she was just 14 years old, she always puts the interests of her planet above her own.

ANAKIN SKYWALKER

Anakin is a boy like no other. A **slave** to the junk dealer **Watto**, he lives with his mother on the **Outer Rim planet of Tatooine**. He has many exceptional talents: the ability to build and repair advanced mechanical devices, unusually fast reflexes, and a keen perception. Any Jedi can sense the Force is **amazingly strong** with him.

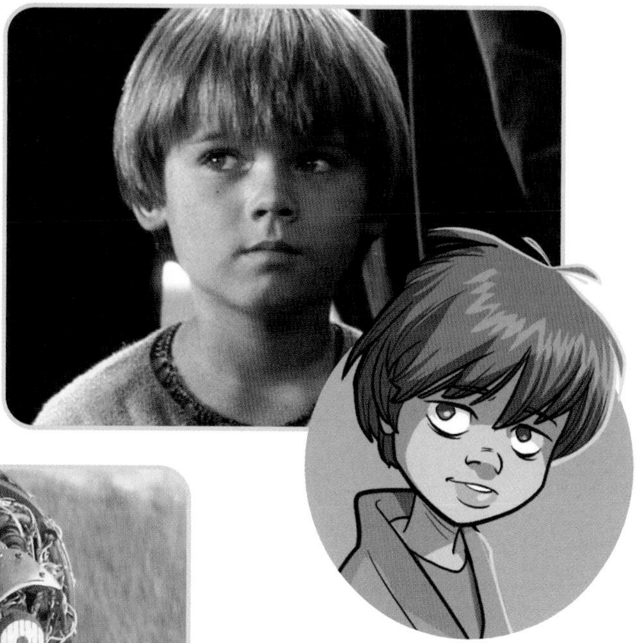

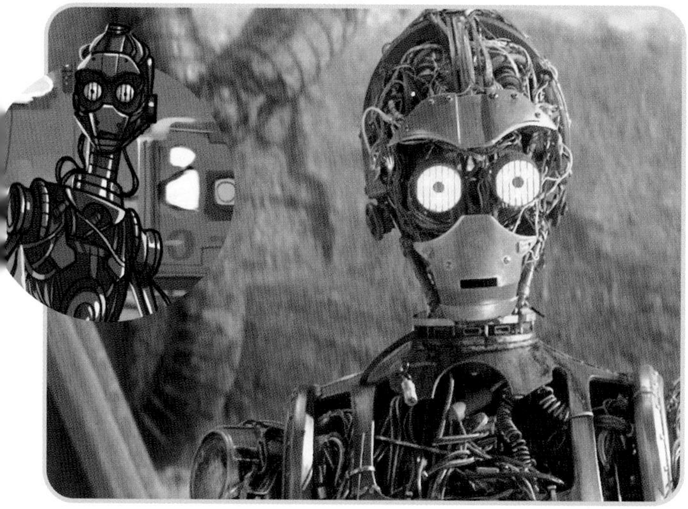

C-3PO

C-3PO is a special **protocol droid**: Anakin rebuilt him from discarded pieces of scrap to help his mother. The droid has no covering, and all his parts are showing.

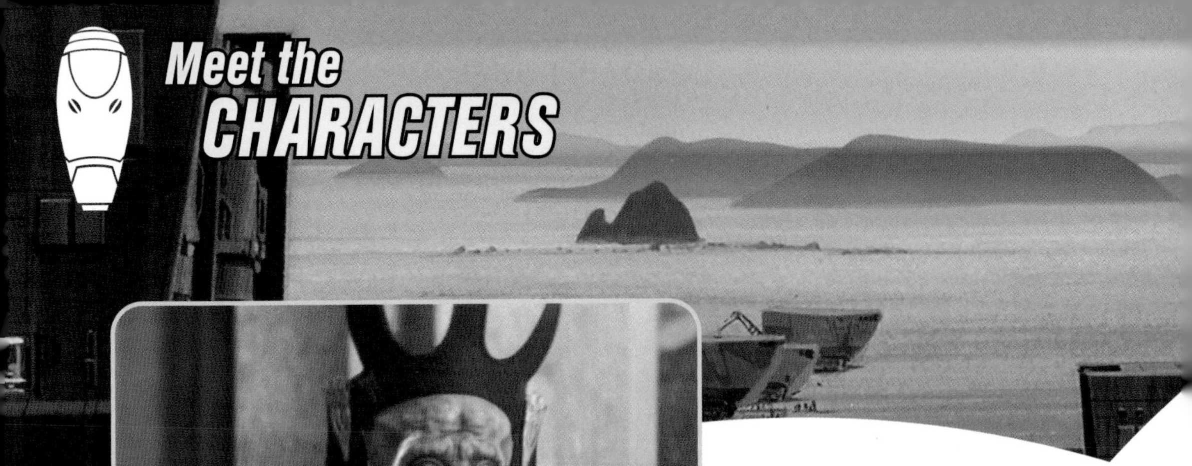

Meet the CHARACTERS

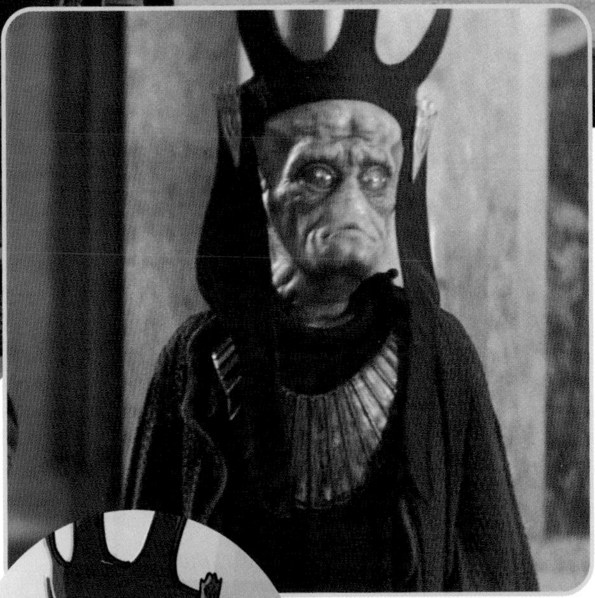

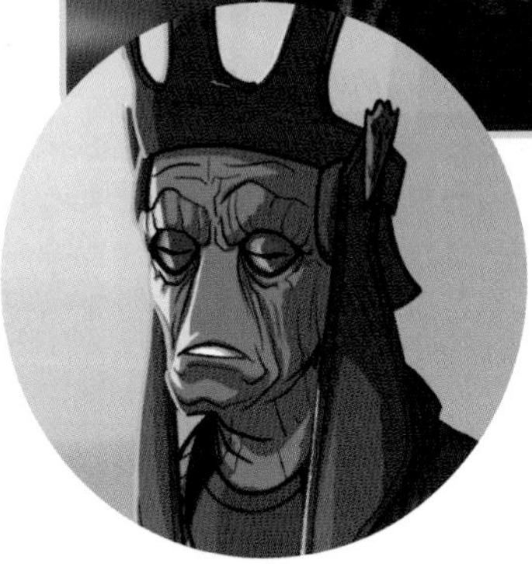

NUTE GUNRAY

The **Commanding Viceroy of the Trade Federation** is a ruthless and deceitful **Neimoidian**. He and the Trade Federation executive board would do anything to increase their power and profit, including making an alliance with a **Sith Lord** and planning the invasion of Naboo.

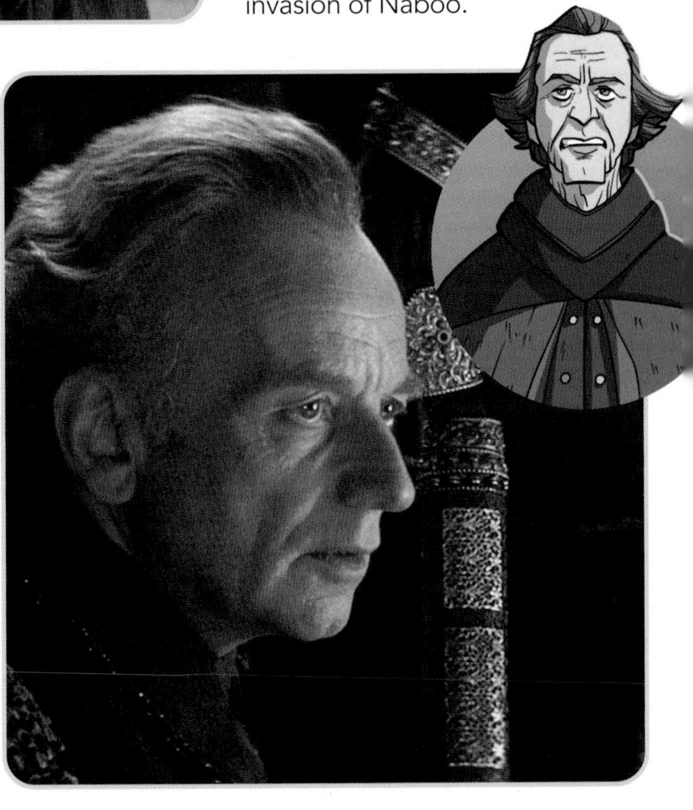

SENATOR PALPATINE

Patience and persistence are Palpatine's greatest talents. Born on the planet Naboo, Palpatine serves in the **Galactic Senate** as the representative of **36 worlds** and he is held in high regard by many fellow senators for his honesty and diplomacy.

DARTH MAUL

Even if he is just the apprentice of the enigmatic **Darth Sidious**, Darth Maul is one of the most dangerous Sith warriors in history. Obedient and loyal to his master, Maul is a deadly agent of the dark side of the Force. Only the bravest Jedi Knight is able to face his powers and his unusual **double-bladed lightsaber**.

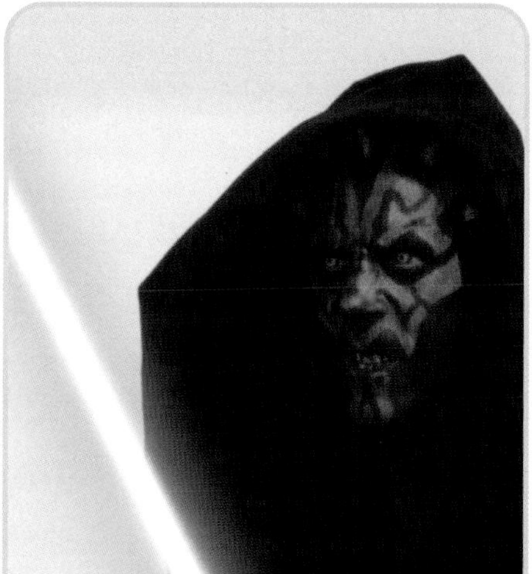

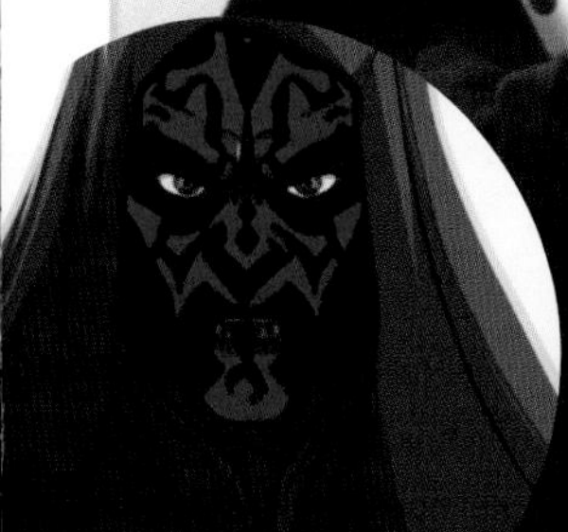

WATTO

Junk dealer and slave owner, Watto only values profit. This **flying Toydarian** lives on Tatooine and is immune to Jedi powers, but he has a weakness: he can't say no to **gambling**, especially when it comes to **podraces**.

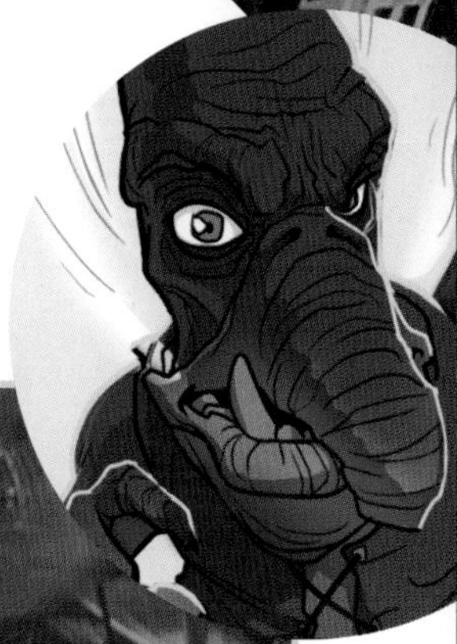

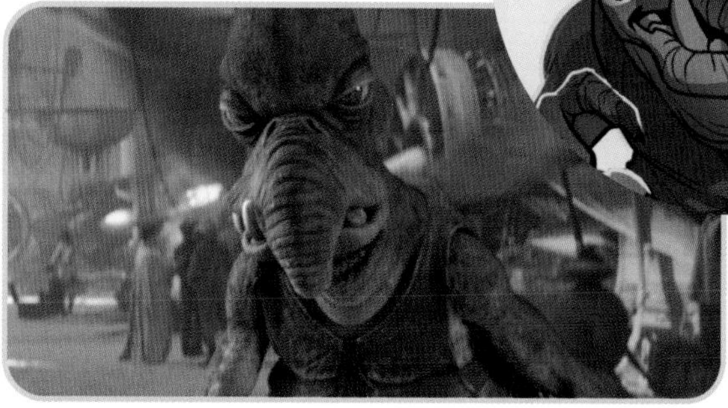

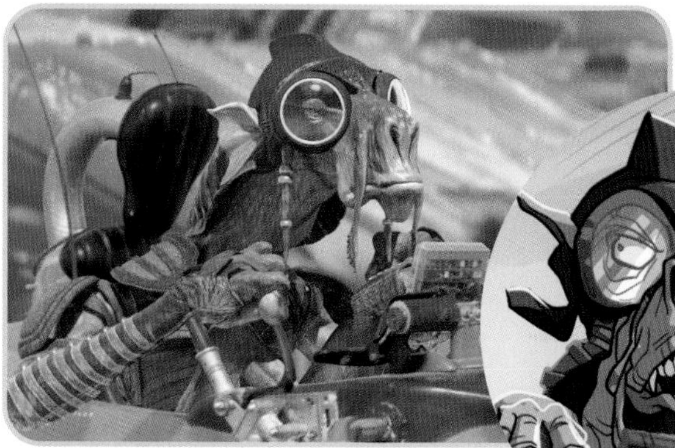

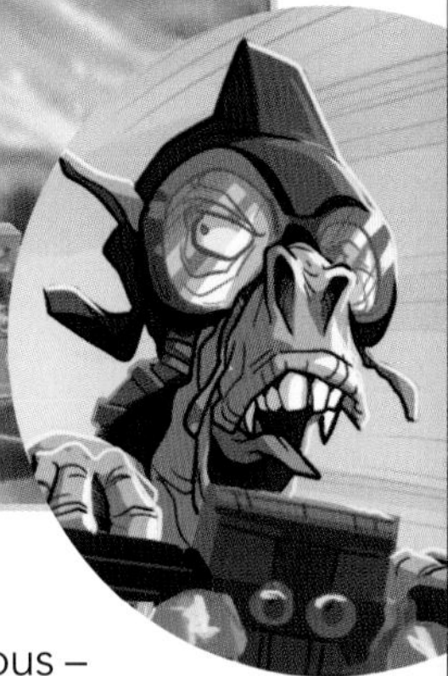

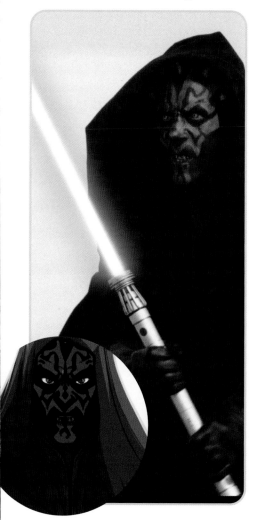

SEBULBA

Sebulba is a famous – and infamous – pilot who never loses a podrace thanks to his **skills**, **resolution**, and **rudeness**. **Cheating** and **tampering** with his opponents' podracers have made him a **champion**, and he has no intention of stopping.

Episode I
THE PHANTOM MENACE

Turmoil has engulfed the Galactic Republic. The taxation of trade routes to outlying star systems is in dispute.

Hoping to resolve the matter with a blockade of deadly battleships, the greedy Trade Federation has stopped all shipping to the small planet of Naboo.

While the Congress of the Republic endlessly debates this alarming chain of events, the Supreme Chancellor has secretly dispatched two Jedi Knights, the guardians of peace and justice in the galaxy, to settle the conflict....

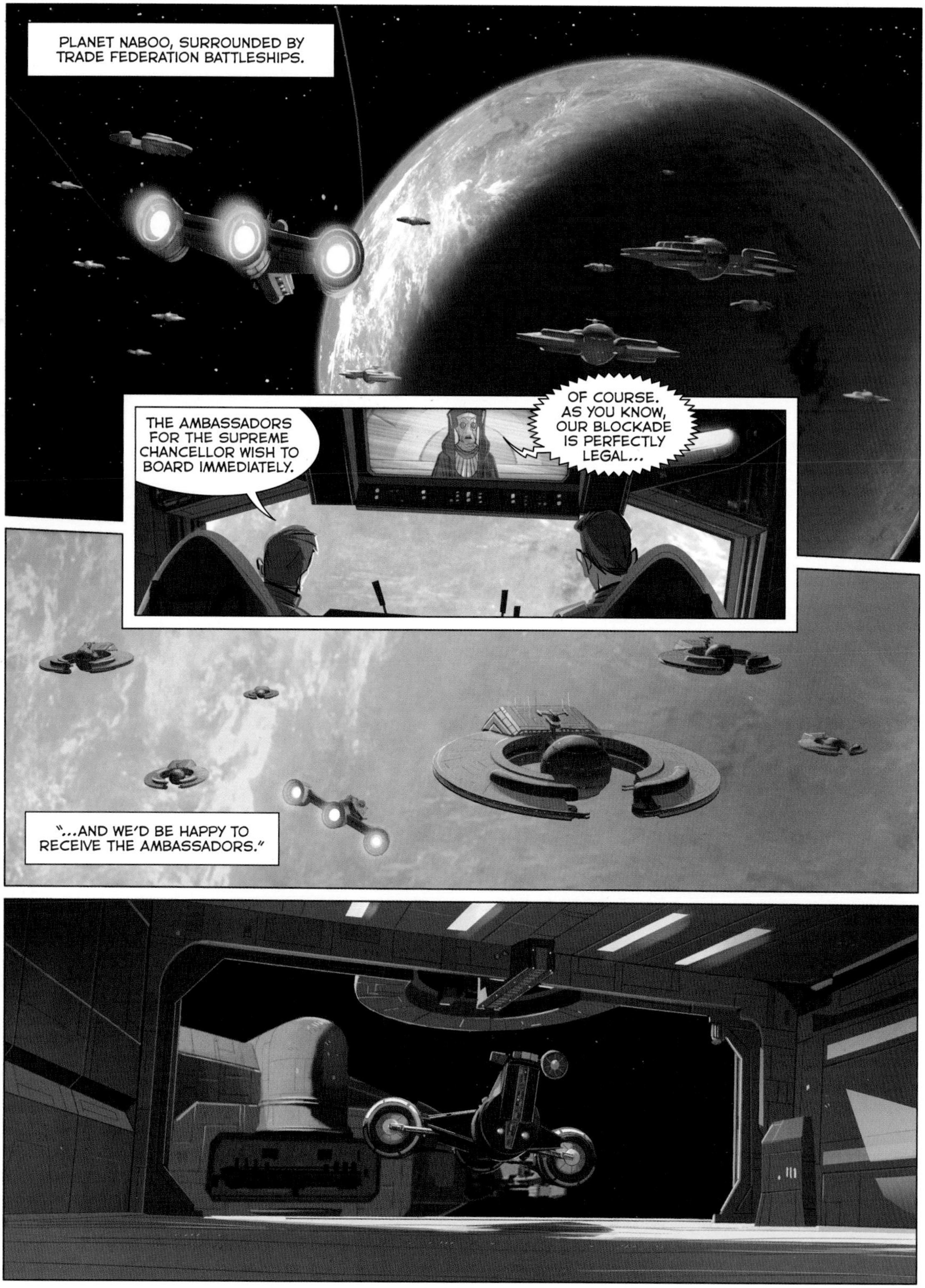
PLANET NABOO, SURROUNDED BY TRADE FEDERATION BATTLESHIPS.
THE AMBASSADORS FOR THE SUPREME CHANCELLOR WISH TO BOARD IMMEDIATELY.
OF COURSE. AS YOU KNOW, OUR BLOCKADE IS PERFECTLY LEGAL...
"...AND WE'D BE HAPPY TO RECEIVE THE AMBASSADORS."

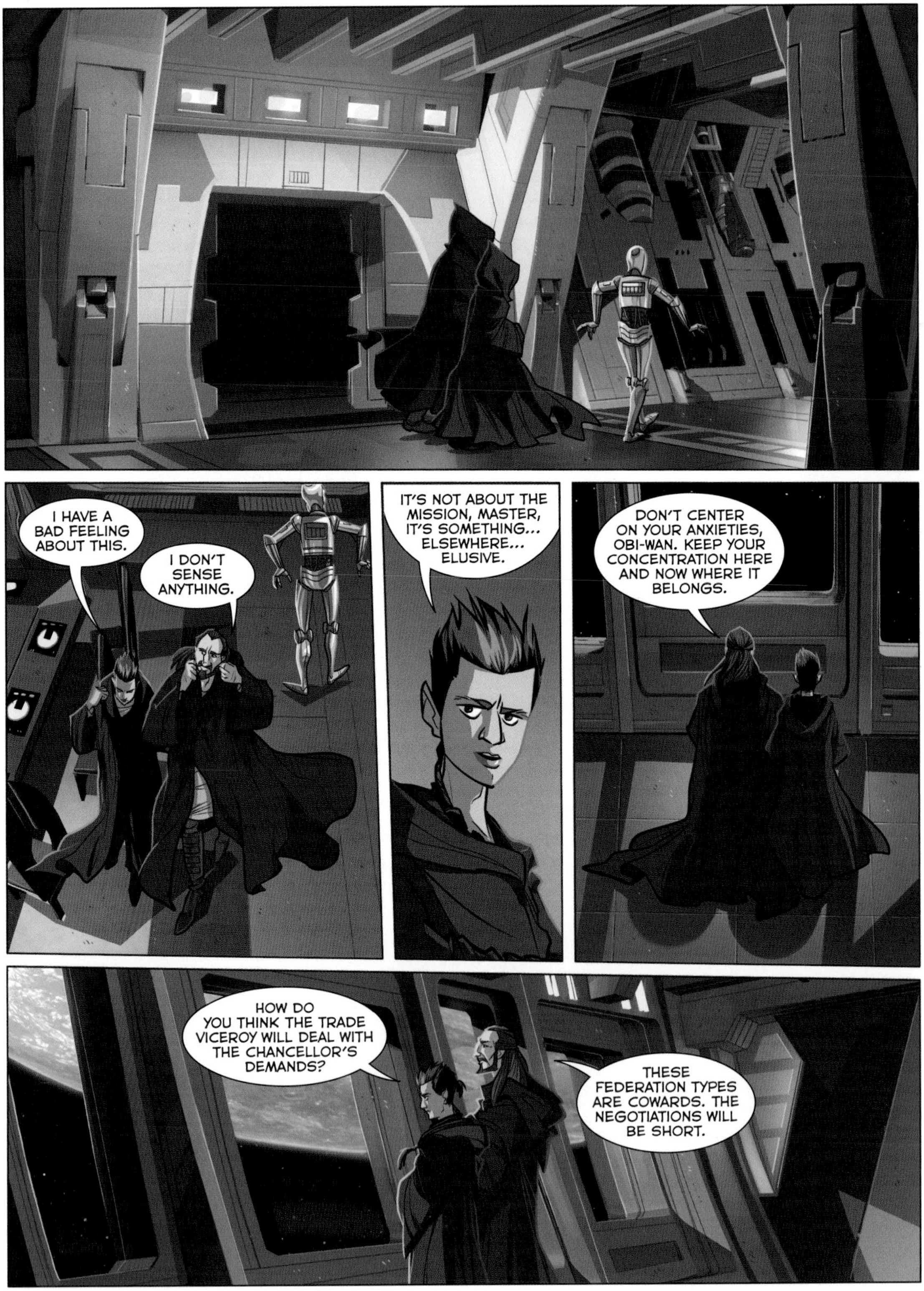
I HAVE A BAD FEELING ABOUT THIS.
I DON'T SENSE ANYTHING.
IT'S NOT ABOUT THE MISSION, MASTER, IT'S SOMETHING... ELSEWHERE... ELUSIVE.
DON'T CENTER ON YOUR ANXIETIES, OBI-WAN. KEEP YOUR CONCENTRATION HERE AND NOW WHERE IT BELONGS.
HOW DO YOU THINK THE TRADE VICEROY WILL DEAL WITH THE CHANCELLOR'S DEMANDS?
THESE FEDERATION TYPES ARE COWARDS. THE NEGOTIATIONS WILL BE SHORT.

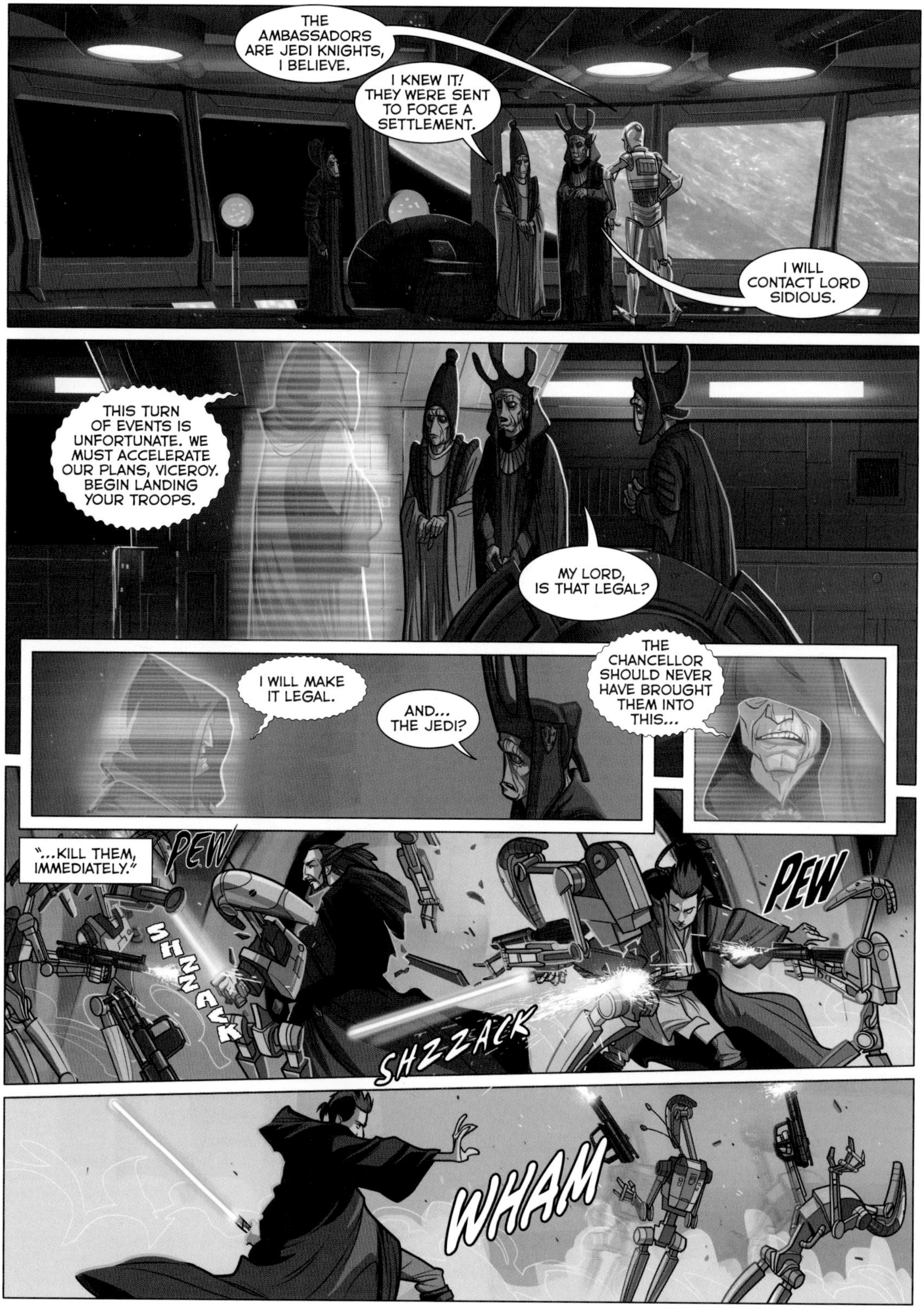
THE AMBASSADORS ARE JEDI KNIGHTS, I BELIEVE.
I KNEW IT! THEY WERE SENT TO FORCE A SETTLEMENT.
I WILL CONTACT LORD SIDIOUS.
THIS TURN OF EVENTS IS UNFORTUNATE. WE MUST ACCELERATE OUR PLANS, VICEROY. BEGIN LANDING YOUR TROOPS.
MY LORD, IS THAT LEGAL?
I WILL MAKE IT LEGAL.
AND... THE JEDI?
THE CHANCELLOR SHOULD NEVER HAVE BROUGHT THEM INTO THIS...
"...KILL THEM, IMMEDIATELY."
PEW
SHZZACK
PEW
SHZZACK
WHAM

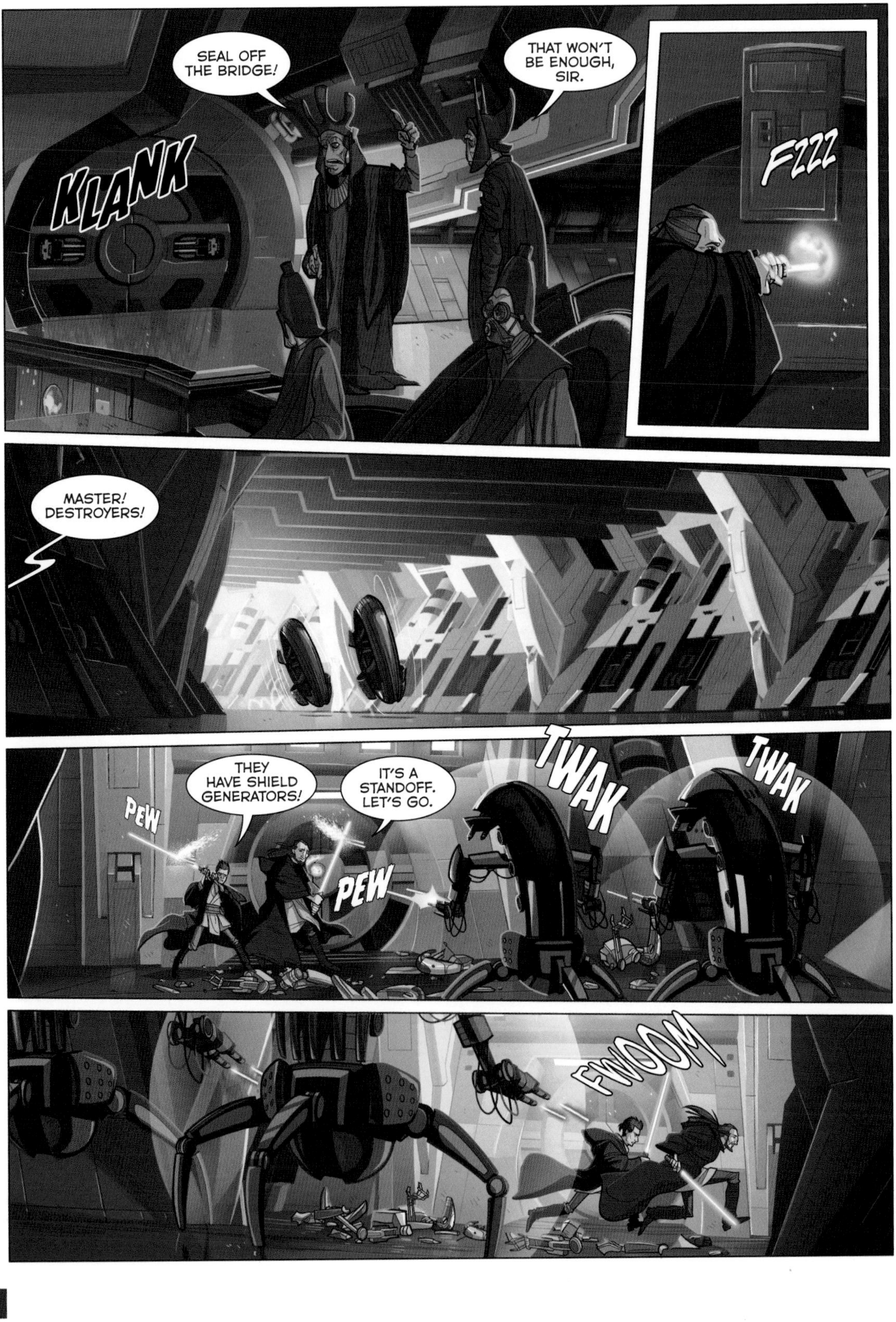

SEAL OFF THE BRIDGE!
KLANK
THAT WON'T BE ENOUGH, SIR.
FZZZ
MASTER! DESTROYERS!
THEY HAVE SHIELD GENERATORS!
IT'S A STANDOFF. LET'S GO.
PEW
PEW
TWAK
TWAK
FWOOM

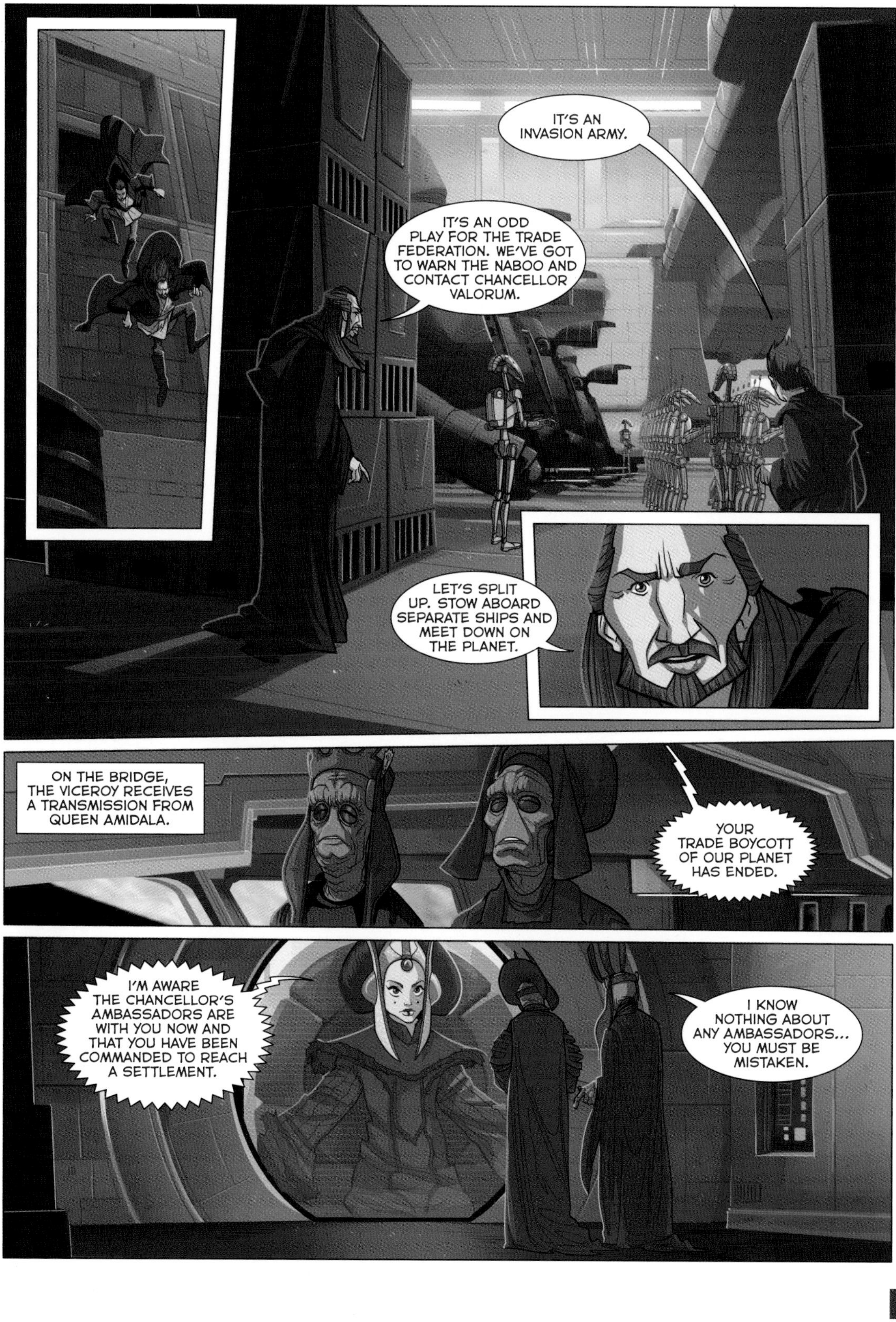
IT'S AN ODD PLAY FOR THE TRADE FEDERATION. WE'VE GOT TO WARN THE NABOO AND CONTACT CHANCELLOR VALORUM.
IT'S AN INVASION ARMY.
LET'S SPLIT UP. STOW ABOARD SEPARATE SHIPS AND MEET DOWN ON THE PLANET.
ON THE BRIDGE, THE VICEROY RECEIVES A TRANSMISSION FROM QUEEN AMIDALA.
YOUR TRADE BOYCOTT OF OUR PLANET HAS ENDED.
I'M AWARE THE CHANCELLOR'S AMBASSADORS ARE WITH YOU NOW AND THAT YOU HAVE BEEN COMMANDED TO REACH A SETTLEMENT.
I KNOW NOTHING ABOUT ANY AMBASSADORS... YOU MUST BE MISTAKEN.

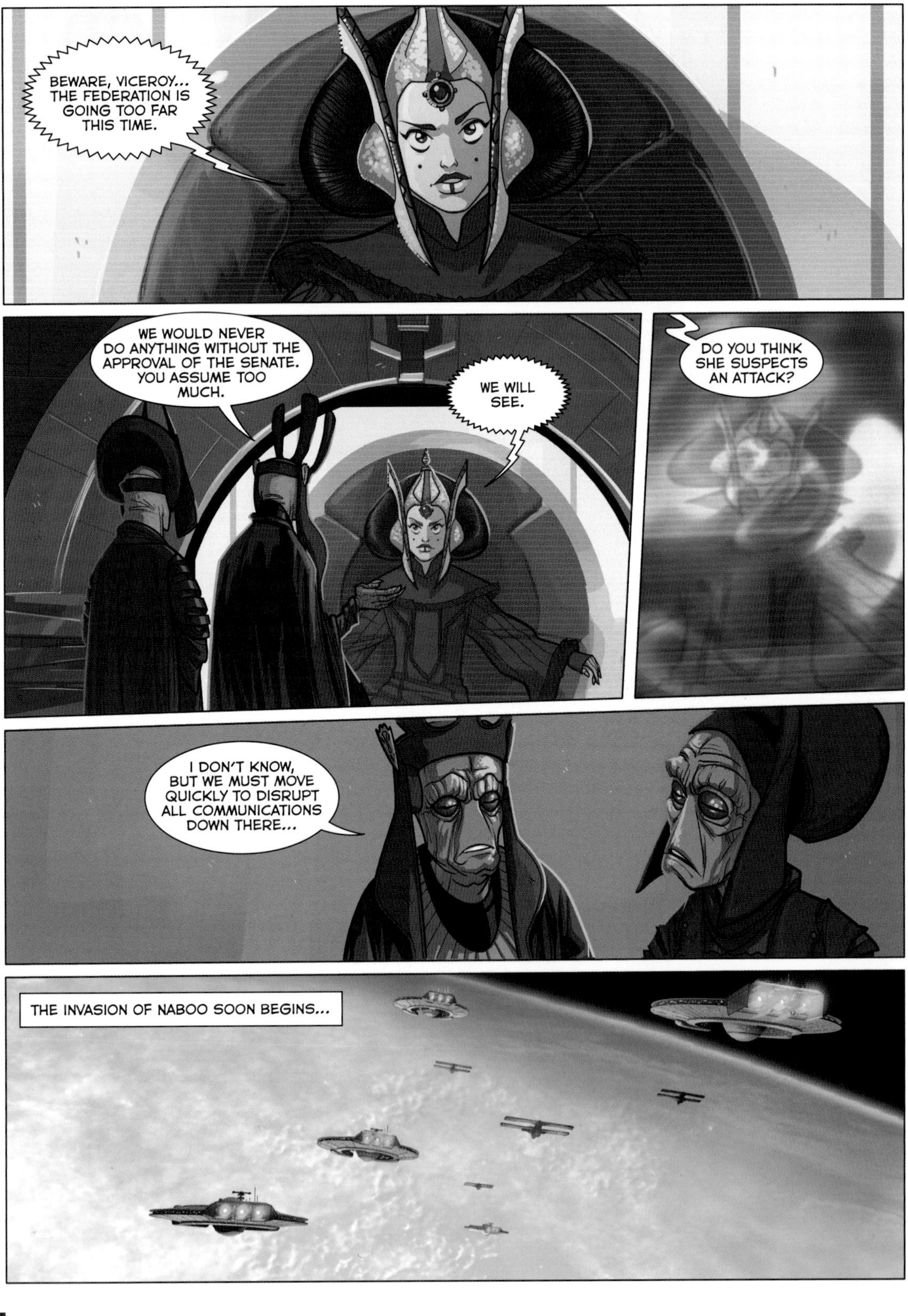
BEWARE, VICEROY... THE FEDERATION IS GOING TOO FAR THIS TIME.
WE WOULD NEVER DO ANYTHING WITHOUT THE APPROVAL OF THE SENATE. YOU ASSUME TOO MUCH.
WE WILL SEE.
DO YOU THINK SHE SUSPECTS AN ATTACK?
I DON'T KNOW, BUT WE MUST MOVE QUICKLY TO DISRUPT ALL COMMUNICATIONS DOWN THERE...
THE INVASION OF NABOO SOON BEGINS...

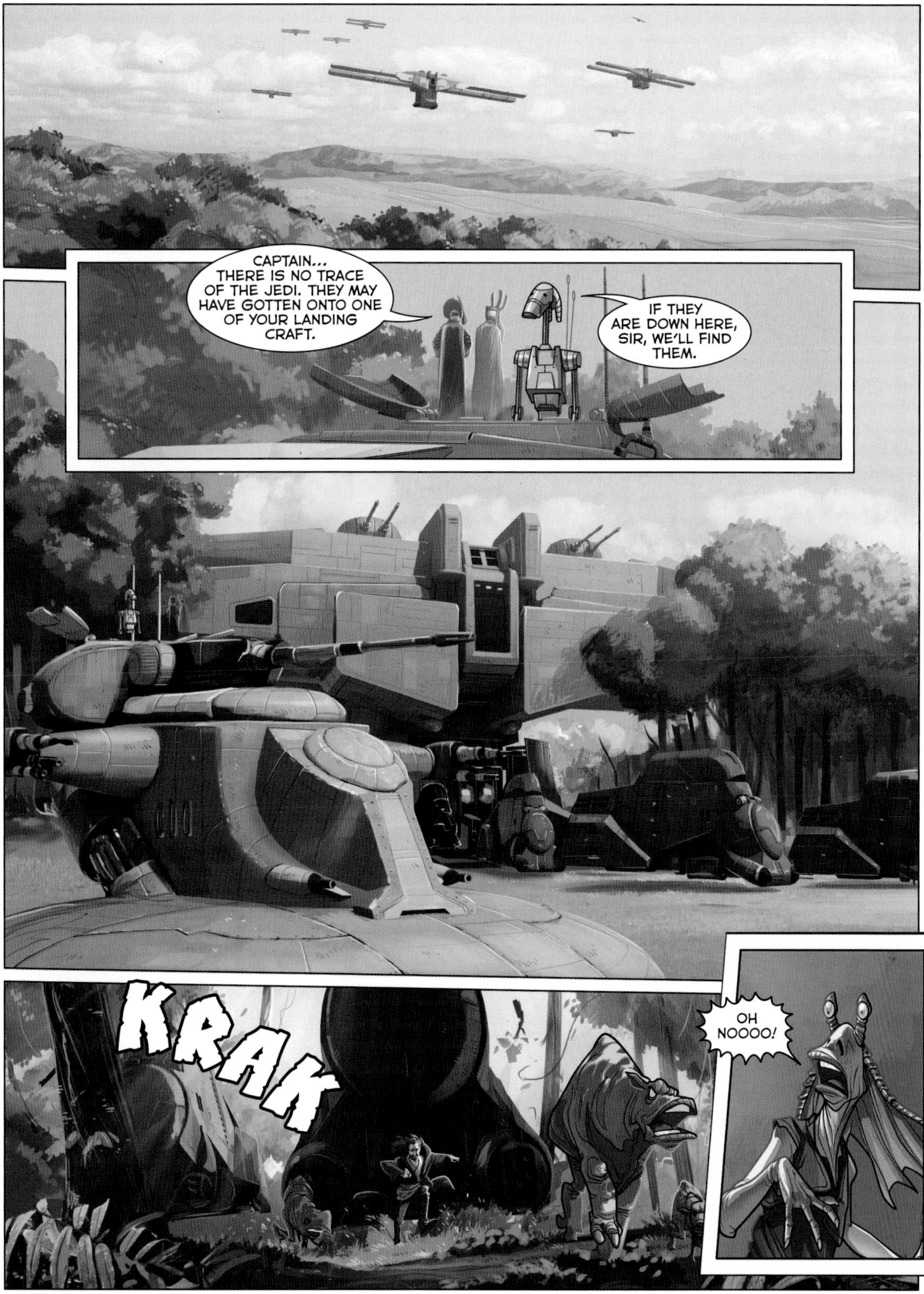
CAPTAIN... THERE IS NO TRACE OF THE JEDI. THEY MAY HAVE GOTTEN ONTO ONE OF YOUR LANDING CRAFT.
IF THEY ARE DOWN HERE, SIR, WE'LL FIND THEM.
KRAK
OH NOOOO!

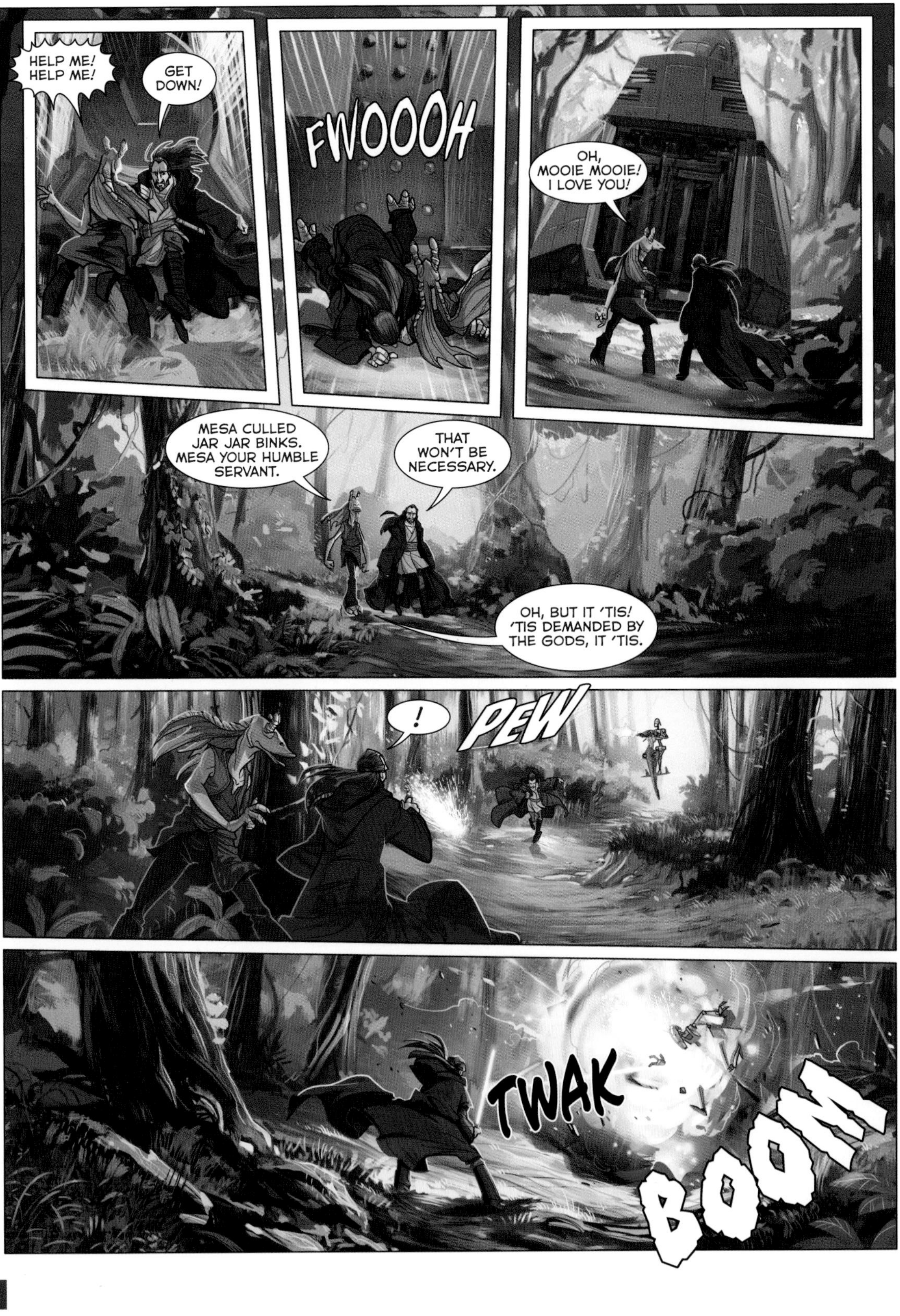
HELP ME! HELP ME!
GET DOWN!
FWOOOH
OH, MOOIE MOOIE! I LOVE YOU!
MESA CULLED JAR JAR BINKS. MESA YOUR HUMBLE SERVANT.
THAT WON'T BE NECESSARY.
OH, BUT IT 'TIS! 'TIS DEMANDED BY THE GODS, IT 'TIS.
!
PEW
TWAK
BOOM

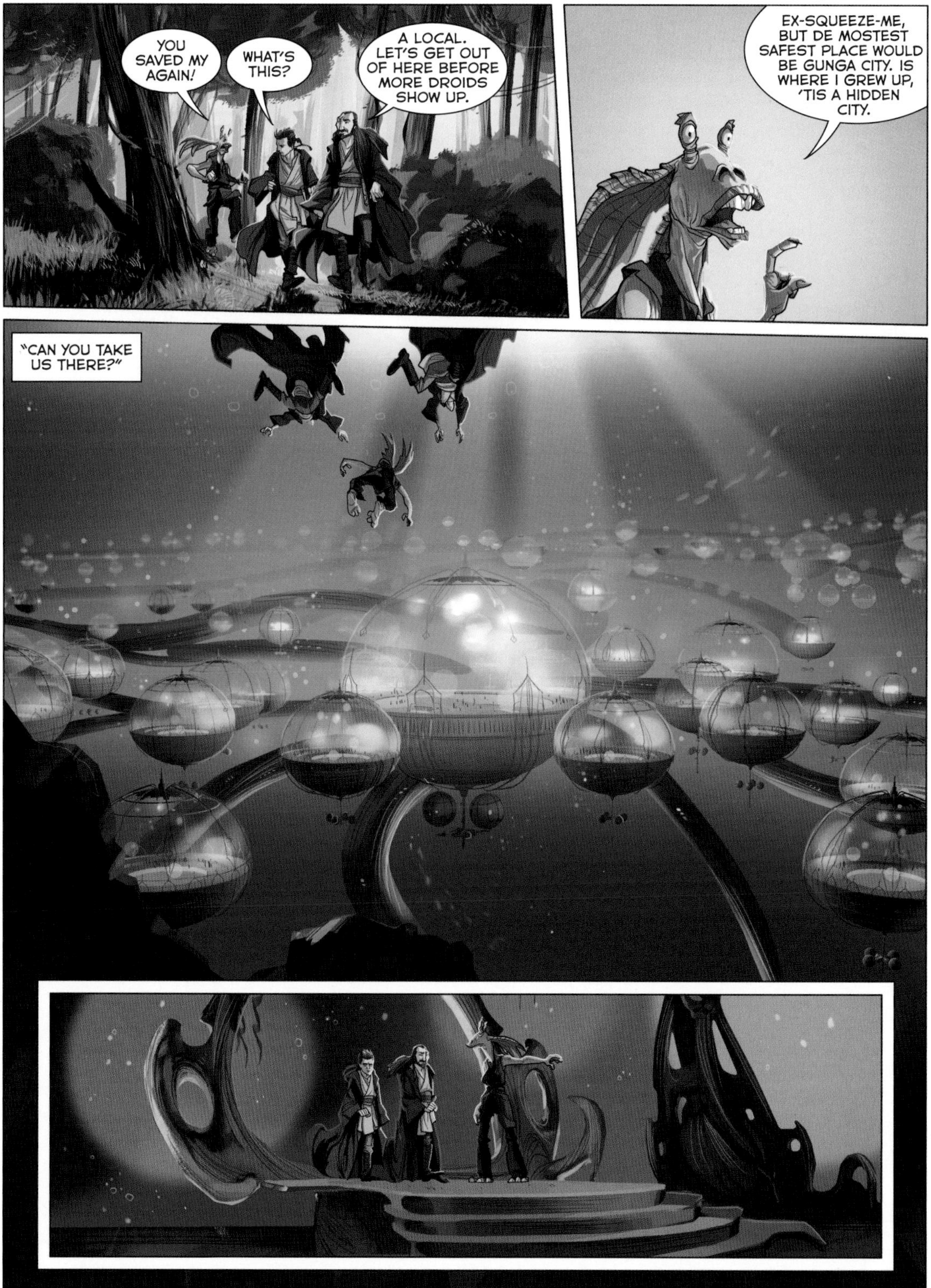
YOU SAVED MY AGAIN!
WHAT'S THIS?
A LOCAL. LET'S GET OUT OF HERE BEFORE MORE DROIDS SHOW UP.
EX-SQUEEZE-ME, BUT DE MOSTEST SAFEST PLACE WOULD BE GUNGA CITY. IS WHERE I GREW UP, 'TIS A HIDDEN CITY.
"CAN YOU TAKE US THERE?"

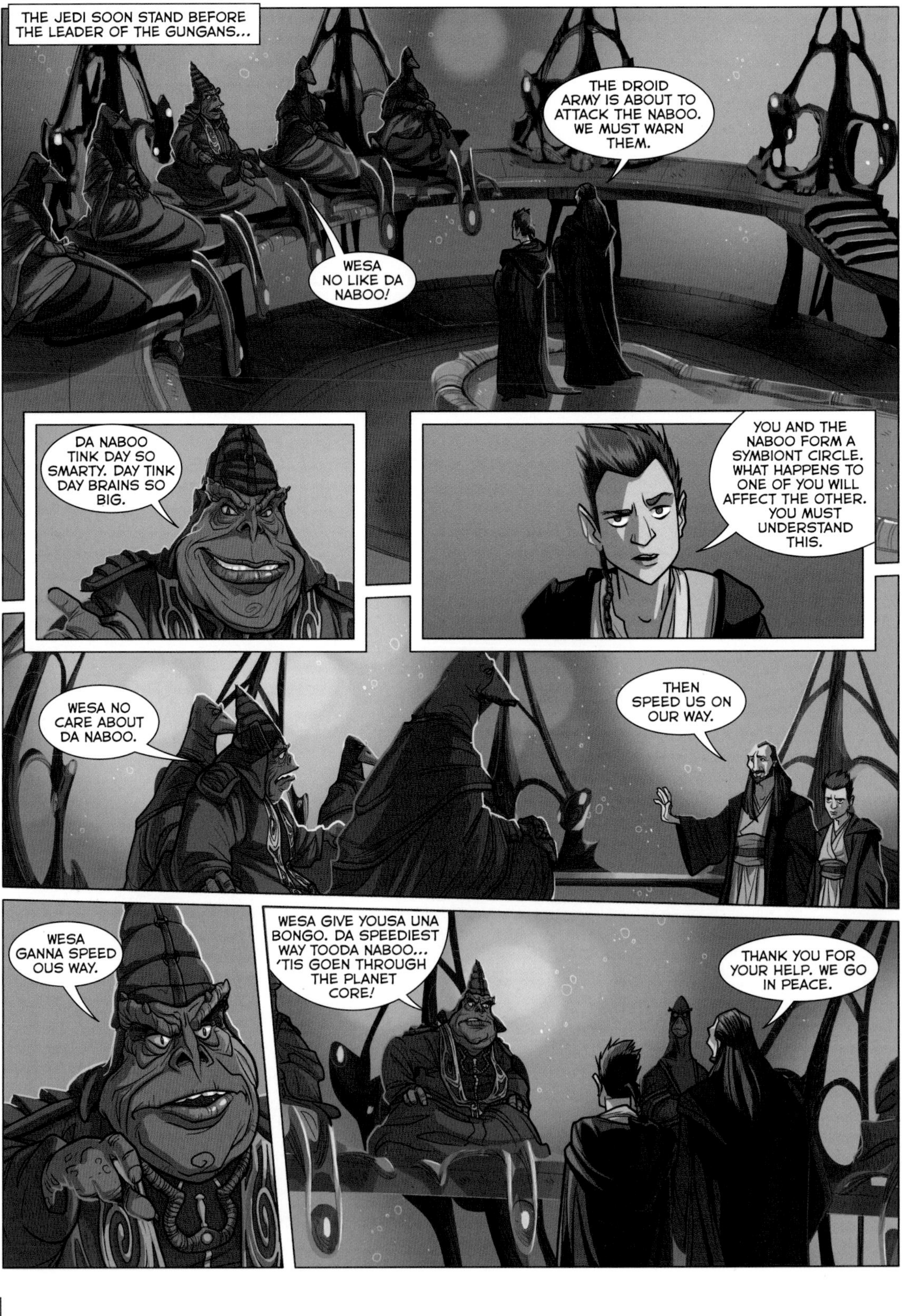
THE JEDI SOON STAND BEFORE THE LEADER OF THE GUNGANS...
THE DROID ARMY IS ABOUT TO ATTACK THE NABOO. WE MUST WARN THEM.
WESA NO LIKE DA NABOO!
DA NABOO TINK DAY SO SMARTY. DAY TINK DAY BRAINS SO BIG.
YOU AND THE NABOO FORM A SYMBIONT CIRCLE. WHAT HAPPENS TO ONE OF YOU WILL AFFECT THE OTHER. YOU MUST UNDERSTAND THIS.
WESA NO CARE ABOUT DA NABOO.
THEN SPEED US ON OUR WAY.
WESA GANNA SPEED OUS WAY.
WESA GIVE YOUSA UNA BONGO. DA SPEEDIEST WAY TOODA NABOO... 'TIS GOEN THROUGH THE PLANET CORE!
THANK YOU FOR YOUR HELP. WE GO IN PEACE.

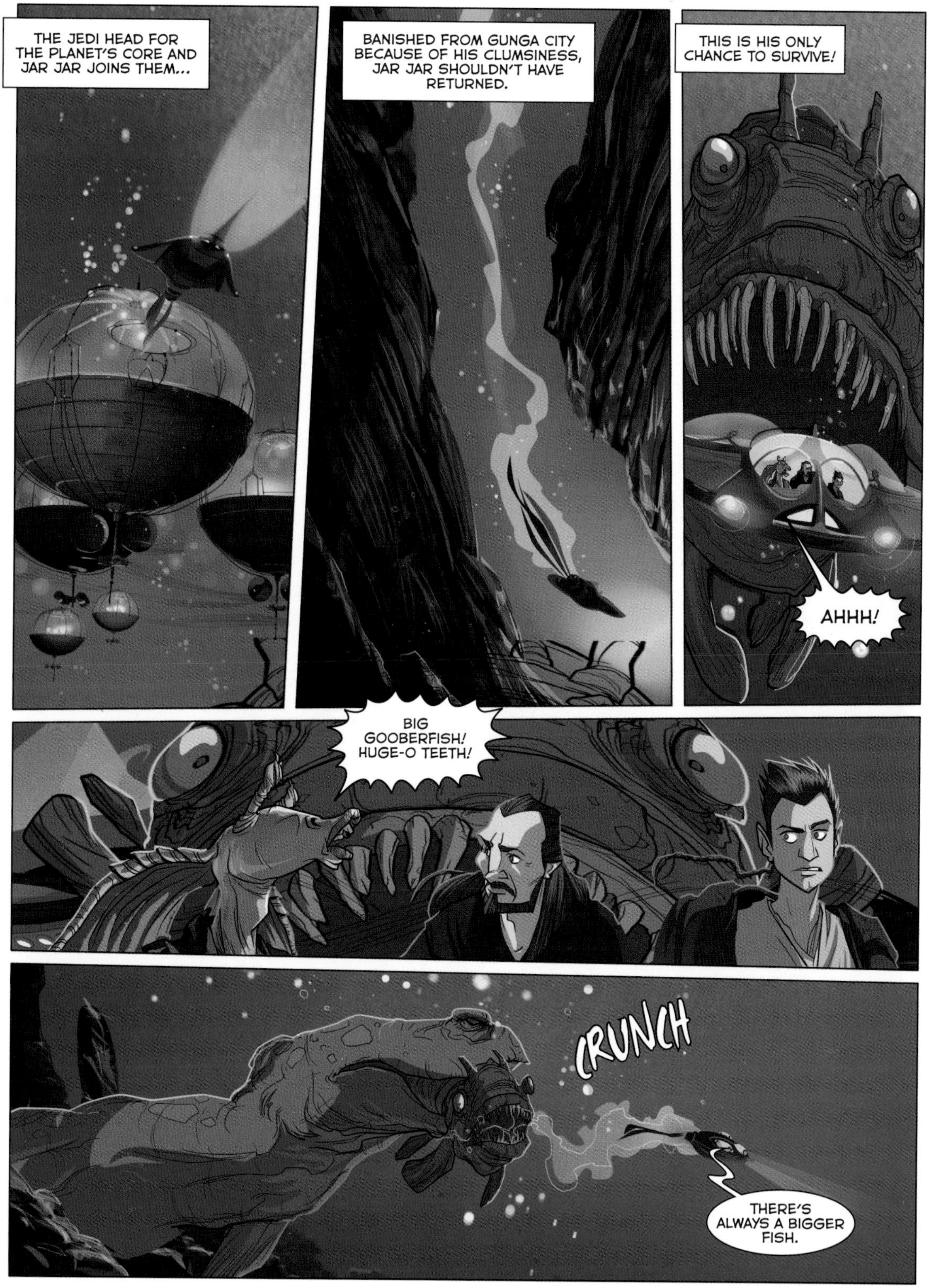
THE JEDI HEAD FOR THE PLANET'S CORE AND JAR JAR JOINS THEM...
BANISHED FROM GUNGA CITY BECAUSE OF HIS CLUMSINESS, JAR JAR SHOULDN'T HAVE RETURNED.
THIS IS HIS ONLY CHANCE TO SURVIVE!
AHHH!
BIG GOOBERFISH! HUGE-O TEETH!
CRUNCH
THERE'S ALWAYS A BIGGER FISH.

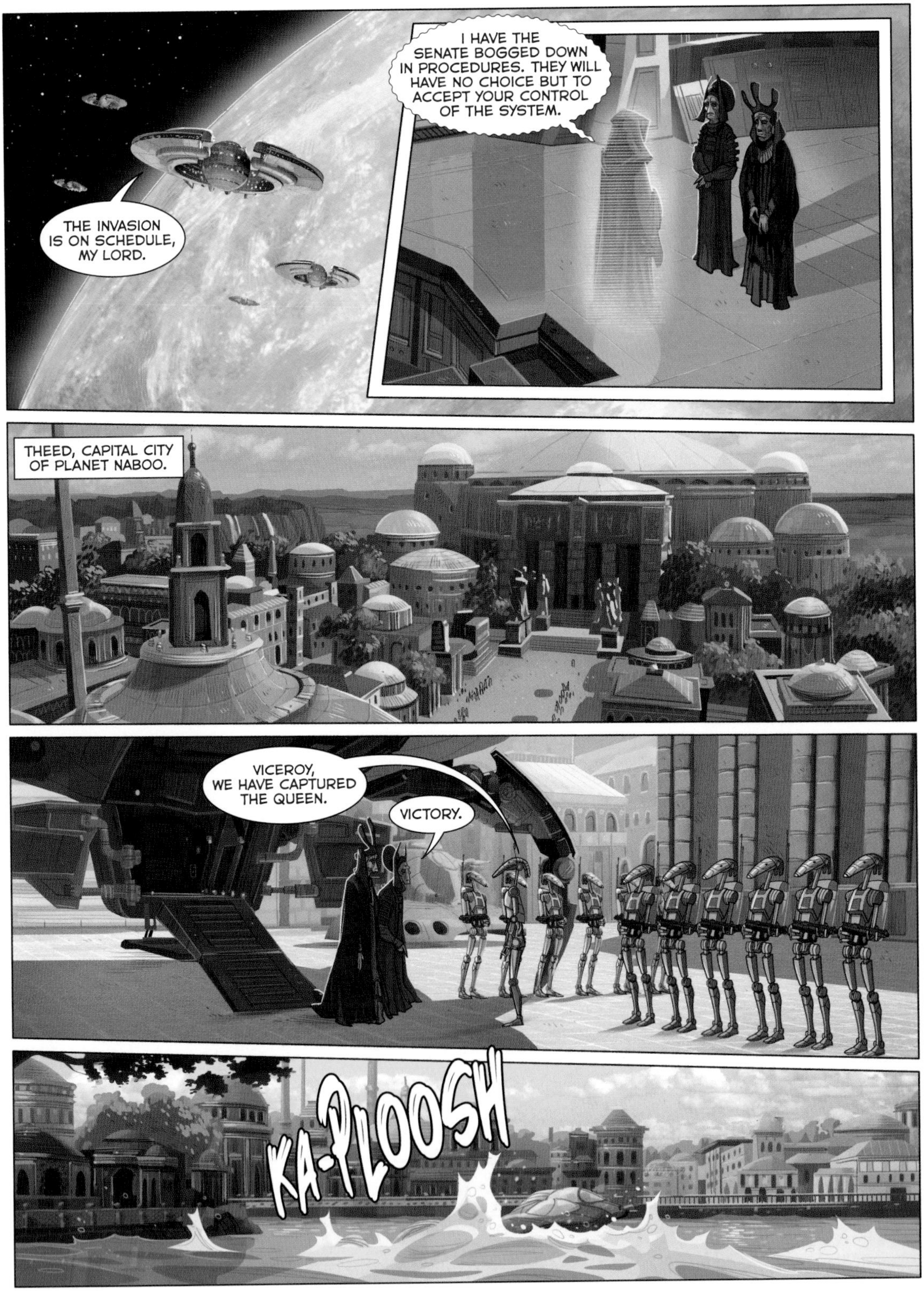
THE INVASION IS ON SCHEDULE, MY LORD.
I HAVE THE SENATE BOGGED DOWN IN PROCEDURES. THEY WILL HAVE NO CHOICE BUT TO ACCEPT YOUR CONTROL OF THE SYSTEM.
THEED, CAPITAL CITY OF PLANET NABOO.
VICEROY, WE HAVE CAPTURED THE QUEEN.
VICTORY.
KA-PLOOSH

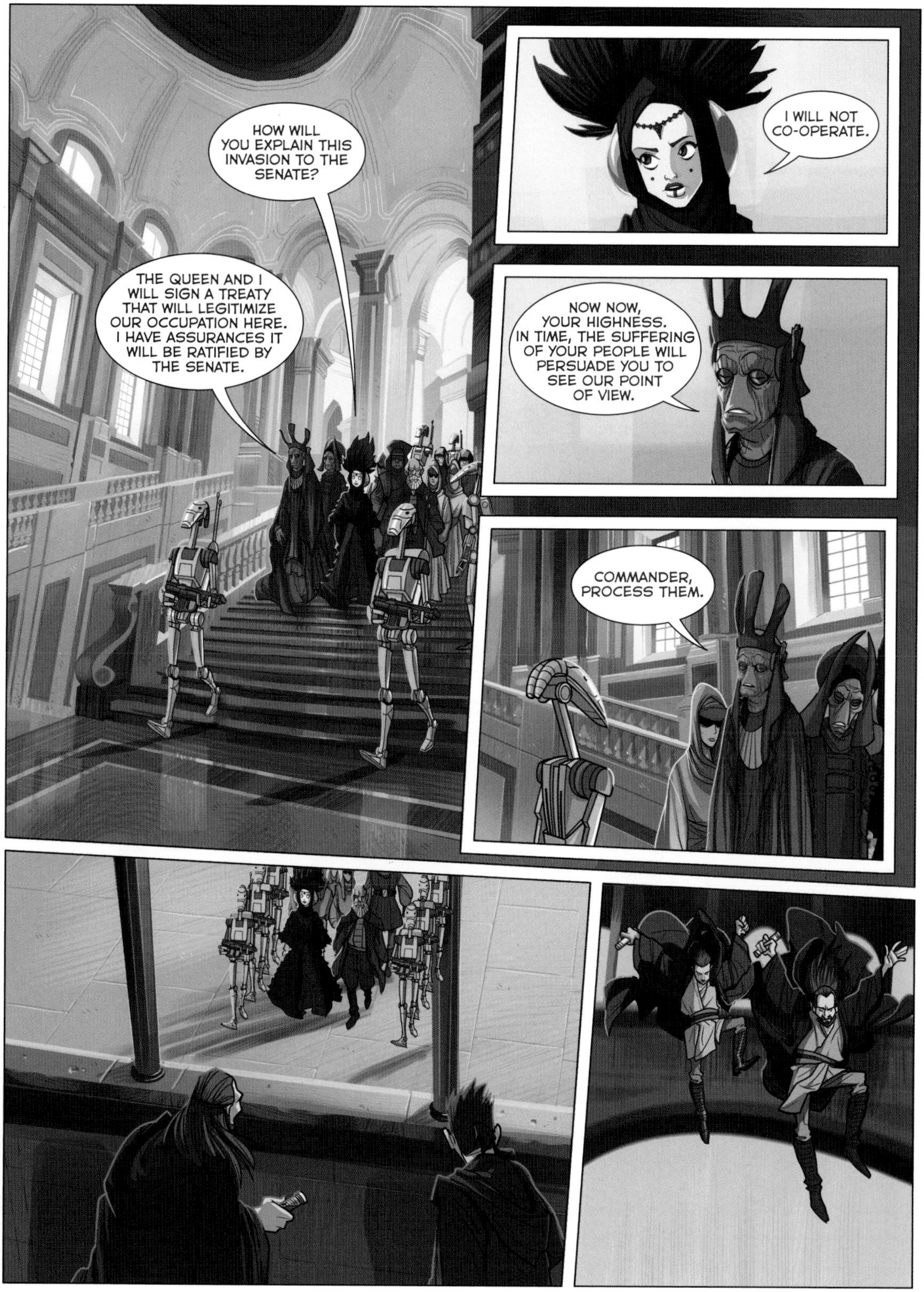
HOW WILL YOU EXPLAIN THIS INVASION TO THE SENATE?
THE QUEEN AND I WILL SIGN A TREATY THAT WILL LEGITIMIZE OUR OCCUPATION HERE. I HAVE ASSURANCES IT WILL BE RATIFIED BY THE SENATE.
I WILL NOT CO-OPERATE.
NOW NOW, YOUR HIGHNESS. IN TIME, THE SUFFERING OF YOUR PEOPLE WILL PERSUADE YOU TO SEE OUR POINT OF VIEW.
COMMANDER, PROCESS THEM.

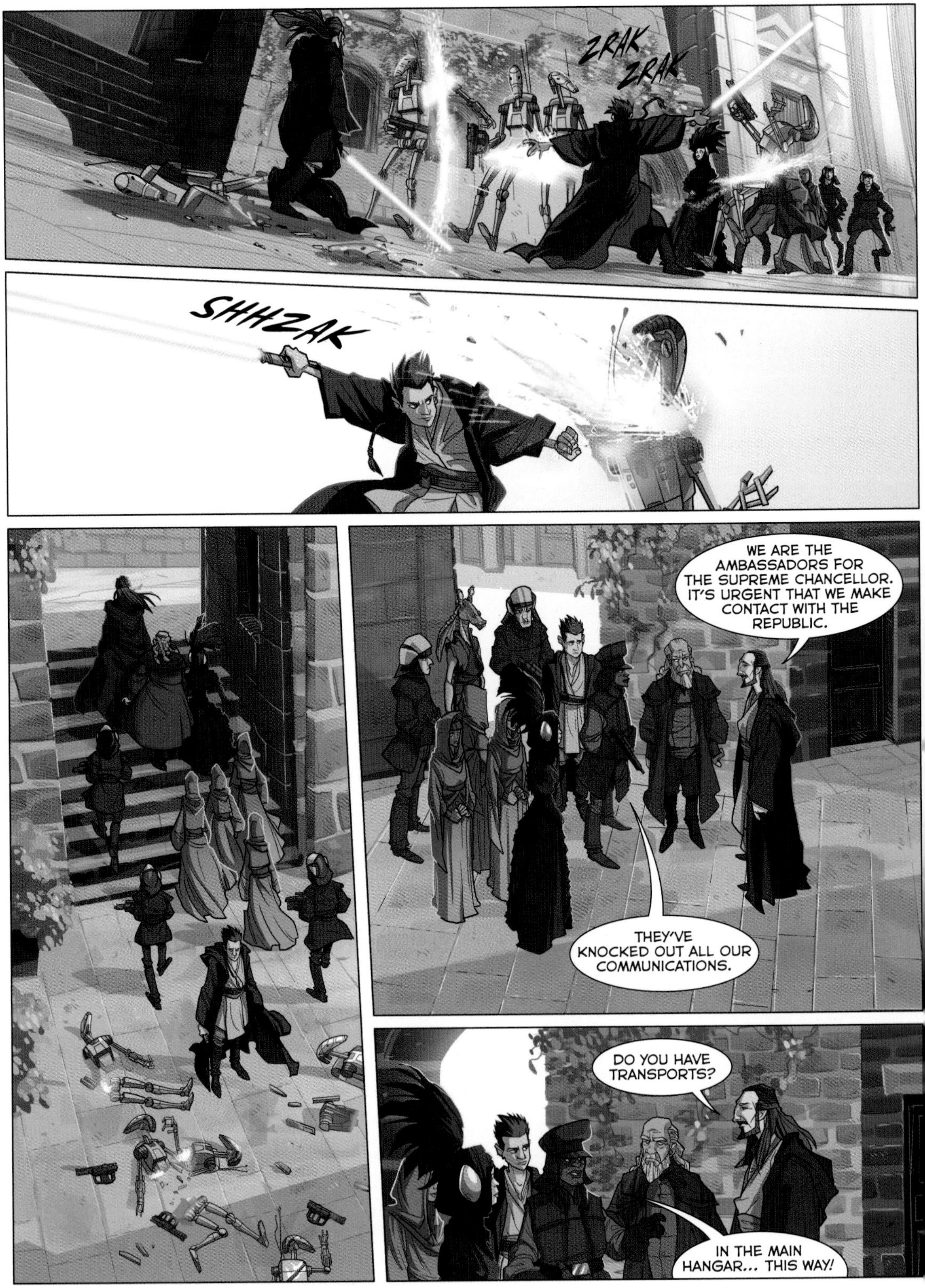
ZRAK
ZRAK
SHHZAK
WE ARE THE AMBASSADORS FOR THE SUPREME CHANCELLOR. IT'S URGENT THAT WE MAKE CONTACT WITH THE REPUBLIC.
THEY'VE KNOCKED OUT ALL OUR COMMUNICATIONS.
DO YOU HAVE TRANSPORTS?
IN THE MAIN HANGAR... THIS WAY!

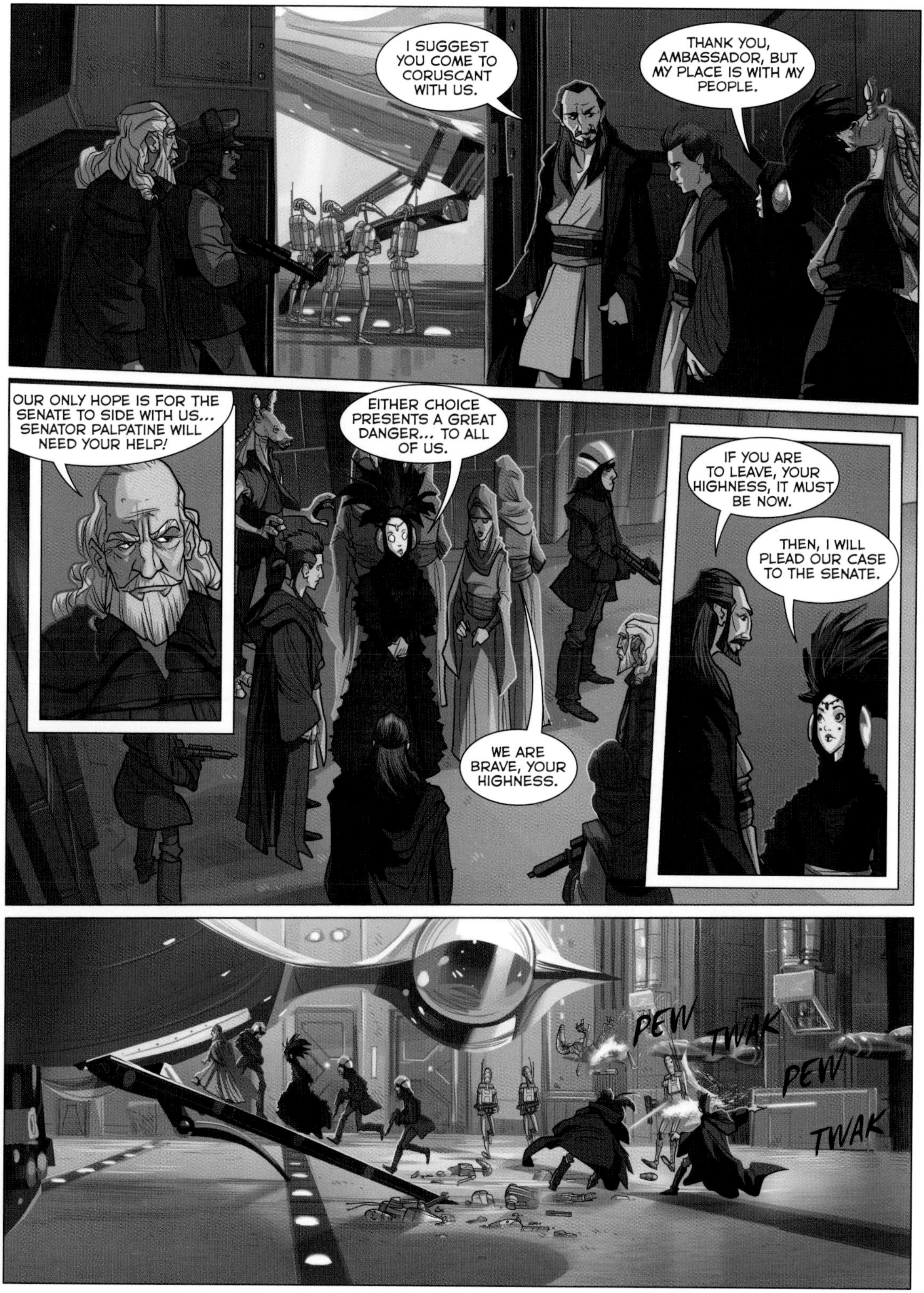
I SUGGEST YOU COME TO CORUSCANT WITH US.
THANK YOU, AMBASSADOR, BUT MY PLACE IS WITH MY PEOPLE.
OUR ONLY HOPE IS FOR THE SENATE TO SIDE WITH US... SENATOR PALPATINE WILL NEED YOUR HELP!
EITHER CHOICE PRESENTS A GREAT DANGER... TO ALL OF US.
WE ARE BRAVE, YOUR HIGHNESS.
IF YOU ARE TO LEAVE, YOUR HIGHNESS, IT MUST BE NOW.
THEN, I WILL PLEAD OUR CASE TO THE SENATE.
PEW
TWAK
PEW
TWAK

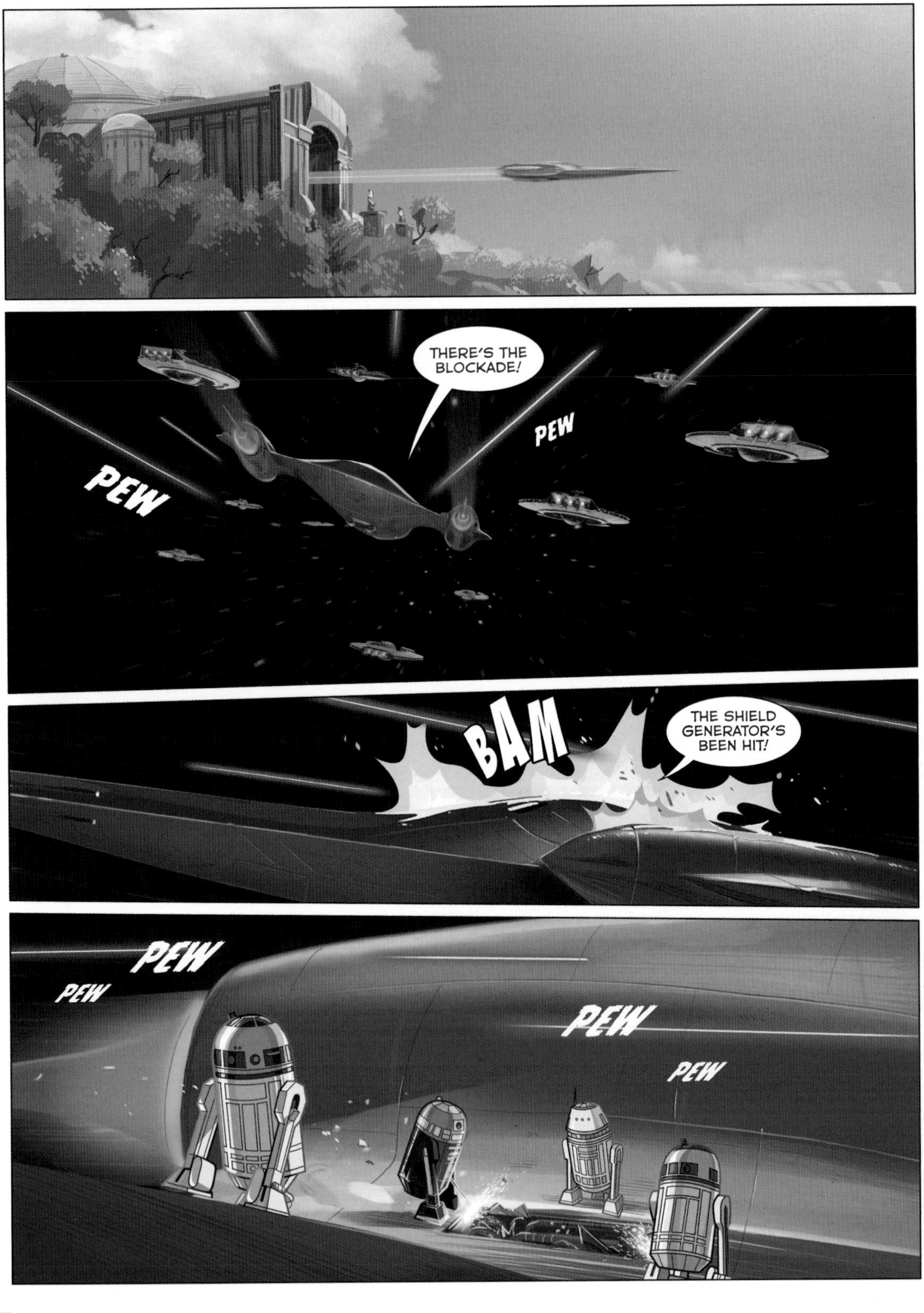
THERE'S THE BLOCKADE!
PEW
PEW
BAM
THE SHIELD GENERATOR'S BEEN HIT!
PEW
PEW
PEW
PEW

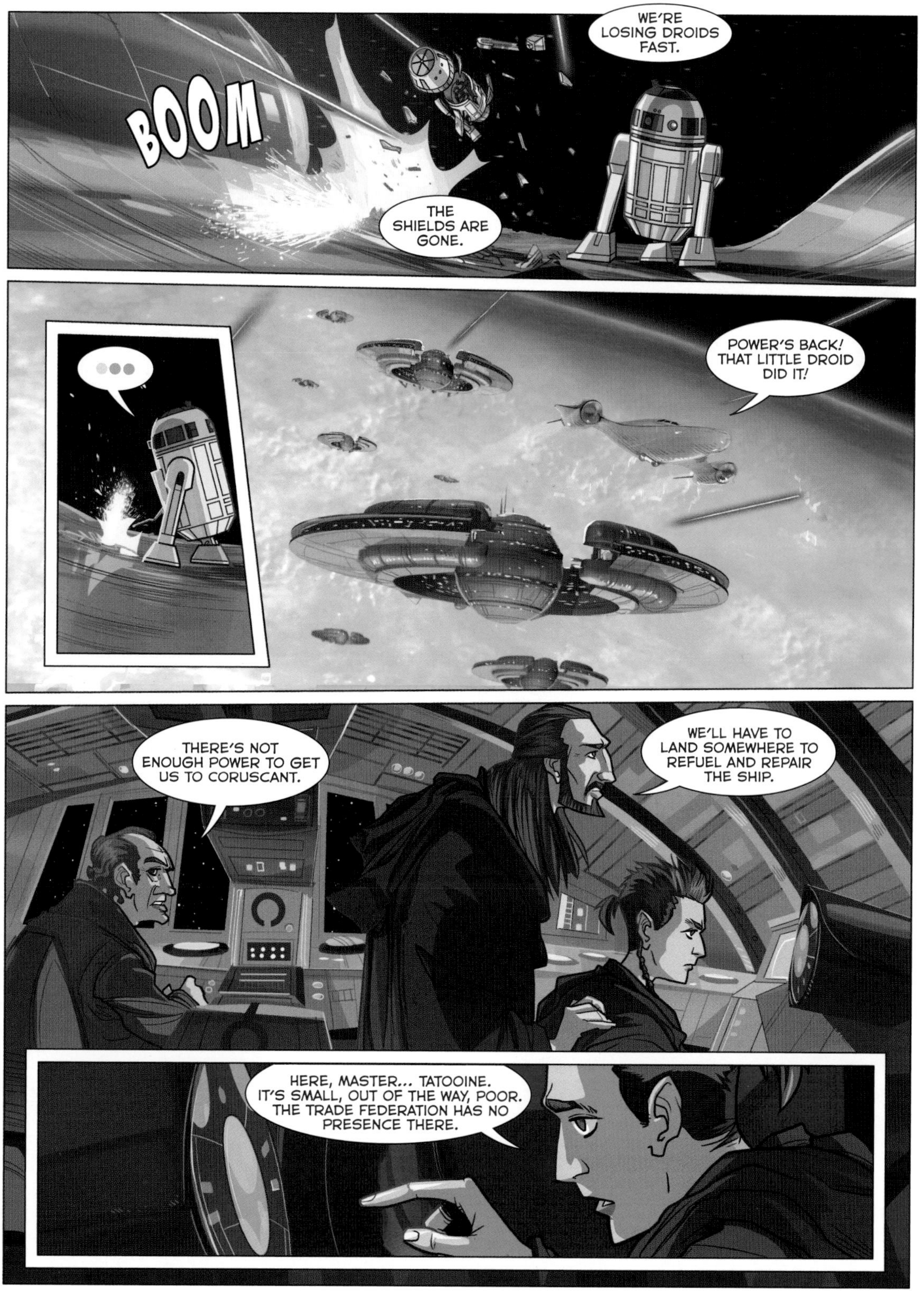
BOOM
WE'RE LOSING DROIDS FAST.
THE SHIELDS ARE GONE.
...
POWER'S BACK! THAT LITTLE DROID DID IT!
THERE'S NOT ENOUGH POWER TO GET US TO CORUSCANT.
WE'LL HAVE TO LAND SOMEWHERE TO REFUEL AND REPAIR THE SHIP.
HERE, MASTER... TATOOINE. IT'S SMALL, OUT OF THE WAY, POOR. THE TRADE FEDERATION HAS NO PRESENCE THERE.

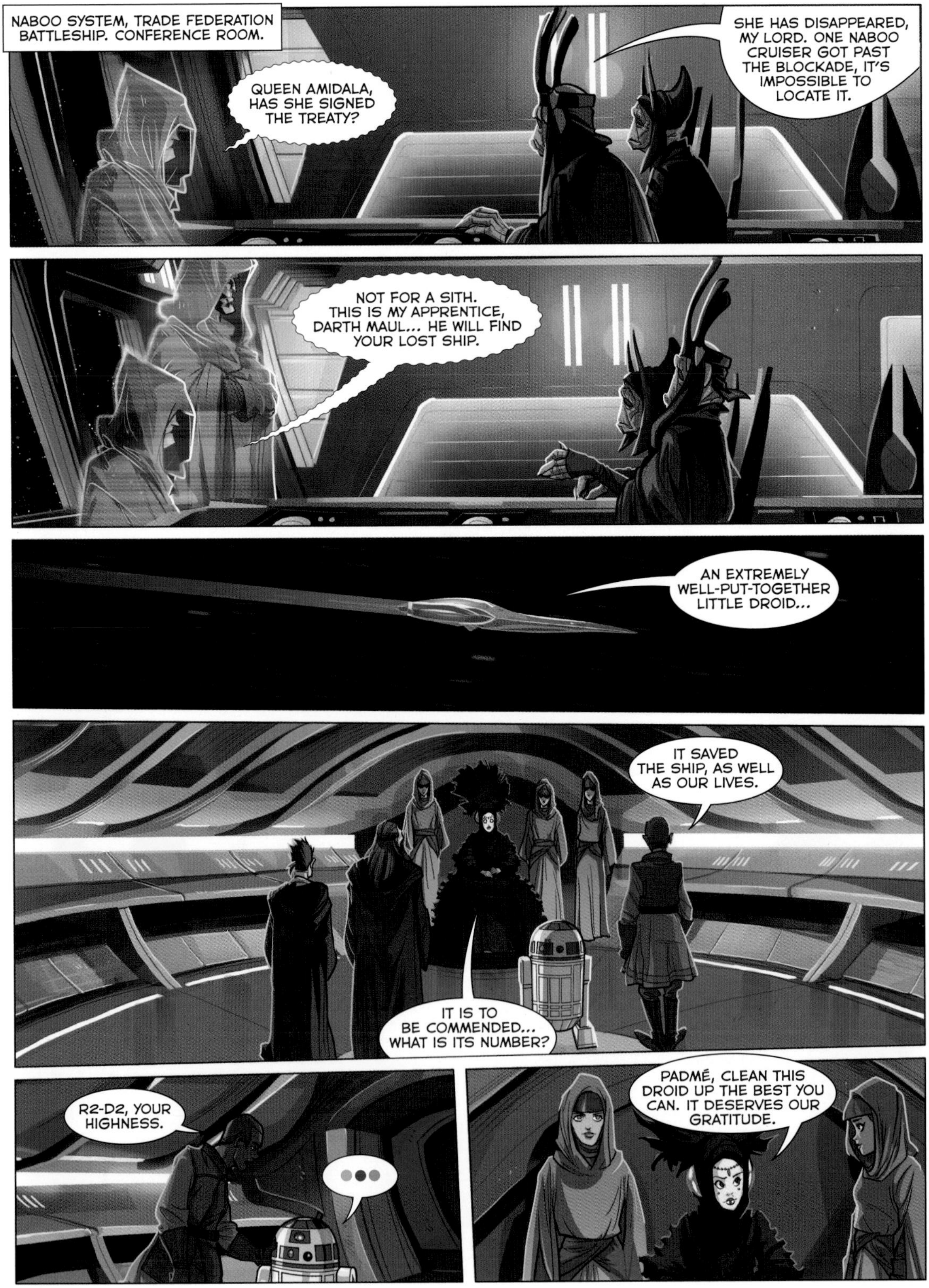
NABOO SYSTEM, TRADE FEDERATION BATTLESHIP. CONFERENCE ROOM.
QUEEN AMIDALA, HAS SHE SIGNED THE TREATY?
SHE HAS DISAPPEARED, MY LORD. ONE NABOO CRUISER GOT PAST THE BLOCKADE, IT'S IMPOSSIBLE TO LOCATE IT.
NOT FOR A SITH. THIS IS MY APPRENTICE, DARTH MAUL... HE WILL FIND YOUR LOST SHIP.
AN EXTREMELY WELL-PUT-TOGETHER LITTLE DROID...
IT SAVED THE SHIP, AS WELL AS OUR LIVES.
IT IS TO BE COMMENDED... WHAT IS ITS NUMBER?
R2-D2, YOUR HIGHNESS.
PADMÉ, CLEAN THIS DROID UP THE BEST YOU CAN. IT DESERVES OUR GRATITUDE.

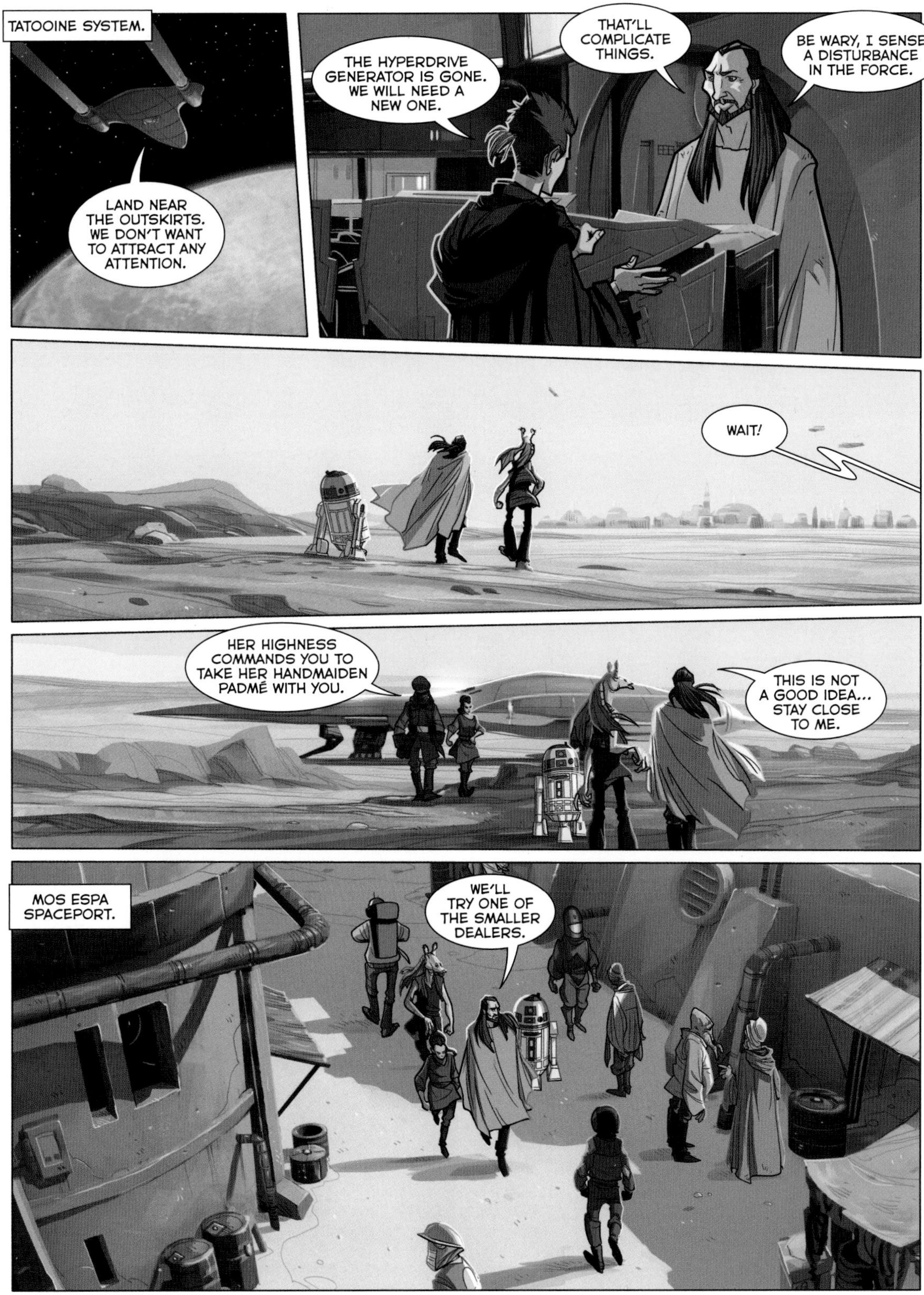
TATOOINE SYSTEM.
LAND NEAR THE OUTSKIRTS. WE DON'T WANT TO ATTRACT ANY ATTENTION.
THE HYPERDRIVE GENERATOR IS GONE. WE WILL NEED A NEW ONE.
THAT'LL COMPLICATE THINGS.
BE WARY, I SENSE A DISTURBANCE IN THE FORCE.
WAIT!
HER HIGHNESS COMMANDS YOU TO TAKE HER HANDMAIDEN PADMÉ WITH YOU.
THIS IS NOT A GOOD IDEA... STAY CLOSE TO ME.
MOS ESPA SPACEPORT.
WE'LL TRY ONE OF THE SMALLER DEALERS.

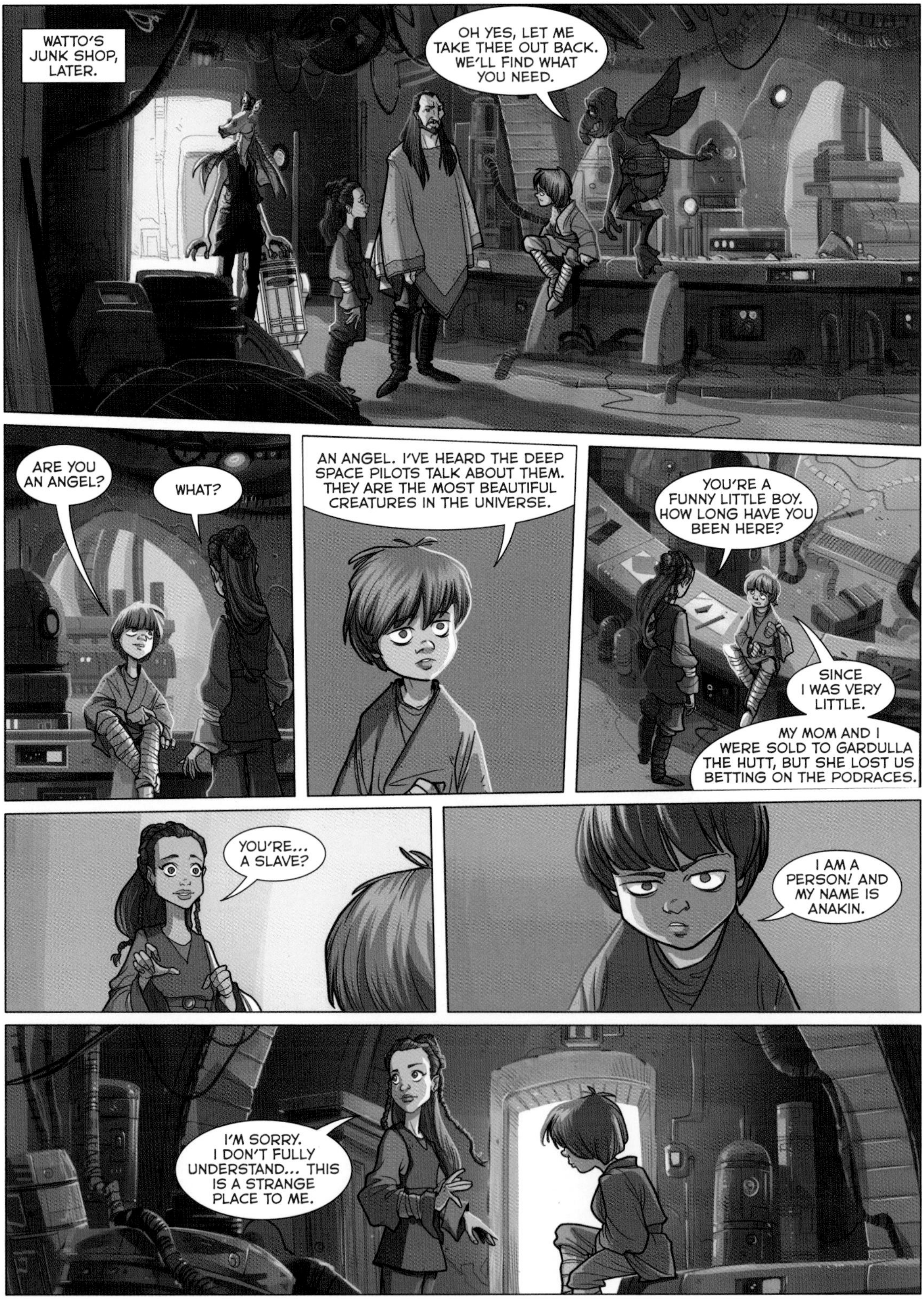
WATTO'S JUNK SHOP, LATER.
OH YES, LET ME TAKE THEE OUT BACK. WE'LL FIND WHAT YOU NEED.
ARE YOU AN ANGEL?
WHAT?
AN ANGEL. I'VE HEARD THE DEEP SPACE PILOTS TALK ABOUT THEM. THEY ARE THE MOST BEAUTIFUL CREATURES IN THE UNIVERSE.
YOU'RE A FUNNY LITTLE BOY. HOW LONG HAVE YOU BEEN HERE?
SINCE I WAS VERY LITTLE.
MY MOM AND I WERE SOLD TO GARDULLA THE HUTT, BUT SHE LOST US BETTING ON THE PODRACES.
YOU'RE... A SLAVE?
I AM A PERSON! AND MY NAME IS ANAKIN.
I'M SORRY. I DON'T FULLY UNDERSTAND... THIS IS A STRANGE PLACE TO ME.

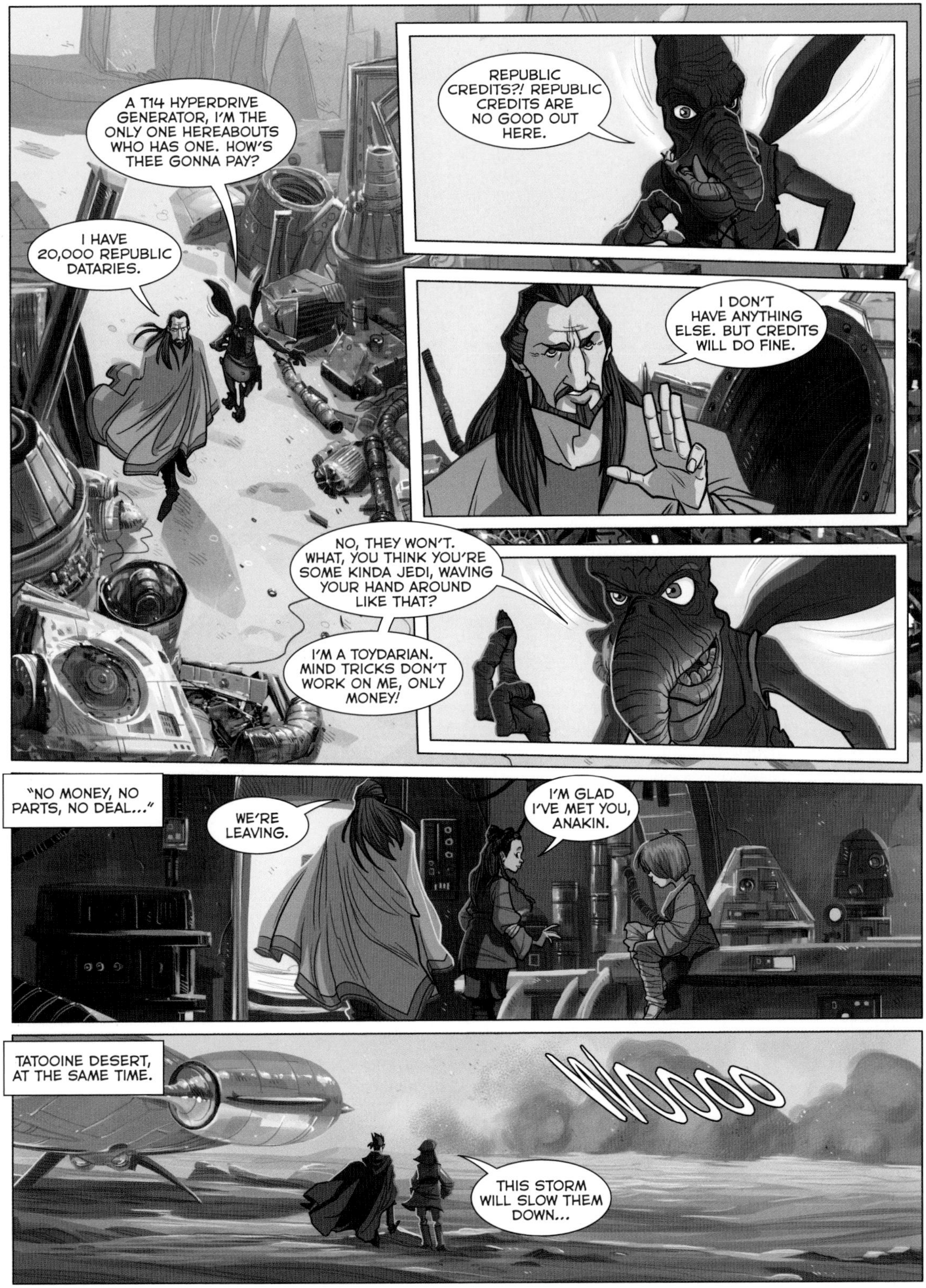
A T14 HYPERDRIVE GENERATOR, I'M THE ONLY ONE HEREABOUTS WHO HAS ONE. HOW'S THEE GONNA PAY?
I HAVE 20,000 REPUBLIC DATARIES.
REPUBLIC CREDITS?! REPUBLIC CREDITS ARE NO GOOD OUT HERE.
I DON'T HAVE ANYTHING ELSE. BUT CREDITS WILL DO FINE.
NO, THEY WON'T. WHAT, YOU THINK YOU'RE SOME KINDA JEDI, WAVING YOUR HAND AROUND LIKE THAT?
I'M A TOYDARIAN. MIND TRICKS DON'T WORK ON ME, ONLY MONEY!
"NO MONEY, NO PARTS, NO DEAL..."
WE'RE LEAVING.
I'M GLAD I'VE MET YOU, ANAKIN.
TATOOINE DESERT, AT THE SAME TIME.
WOOOO
THIS STORM WILL SLOW THEM DOWN...

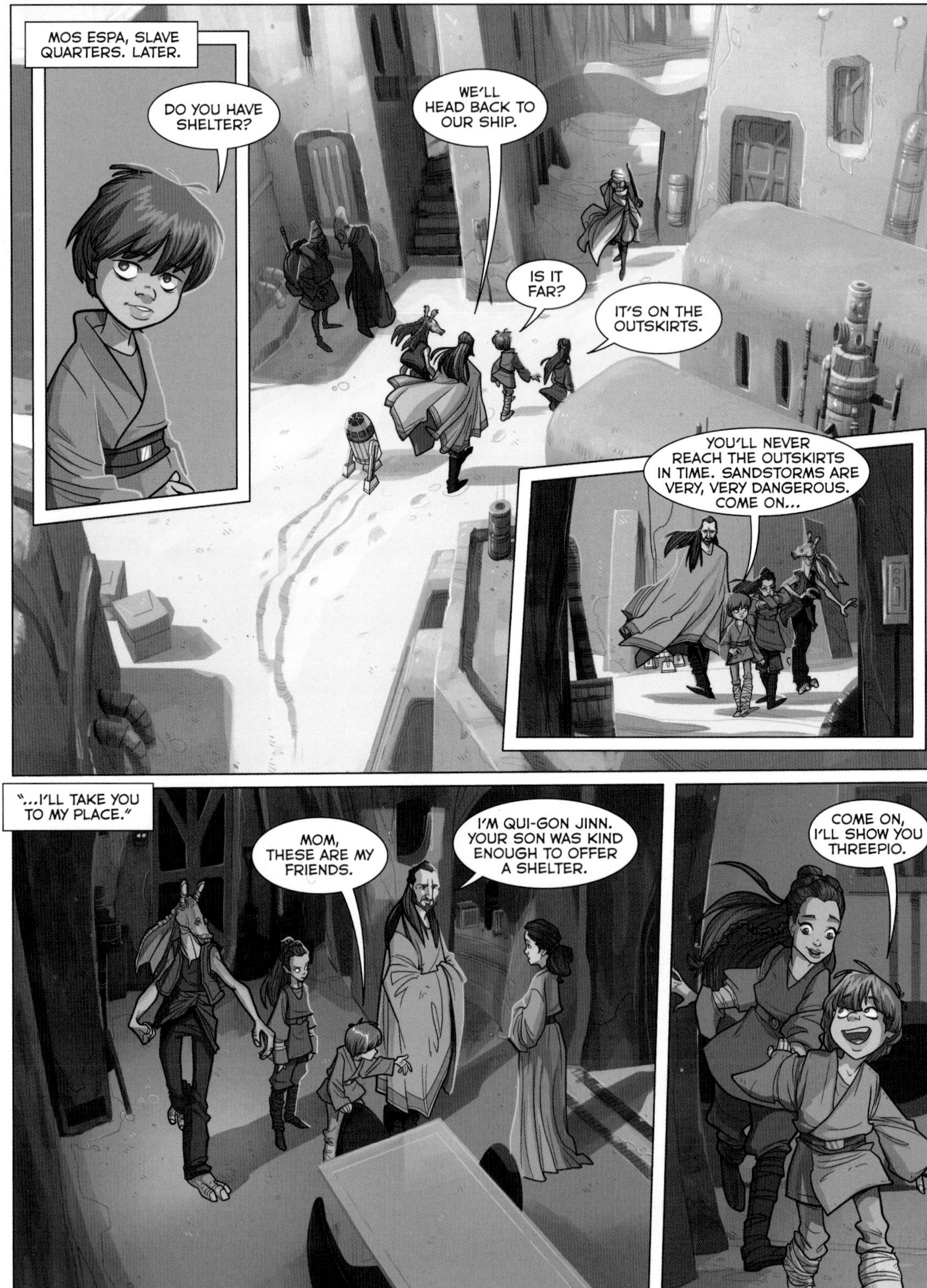
MOS ESPA, SLAVE QUARTERS. LATER.
DO YOU HAVE SHELTER?
WE'LL HEAD BACK TO OUR SHIP.
IS IT FAR?
IT'S ON THE OUTSKIRTS.
YOU'LL NEVER REACH THE OUTSKIRTS IN TIME. SANDSTORMS ARE VERY, VERY DANGEROUS. COME ON...
"...I'LL TAKE YOU TO MY PLACE."
MOM, THESE ARE MY FRIENDS.
I'M QUI-GON JINN. YOUR SON WAS KIND ENOUGH TO OFFER A SHELTER.
COME ON, I'LL SHOW YOU THREEPIO.

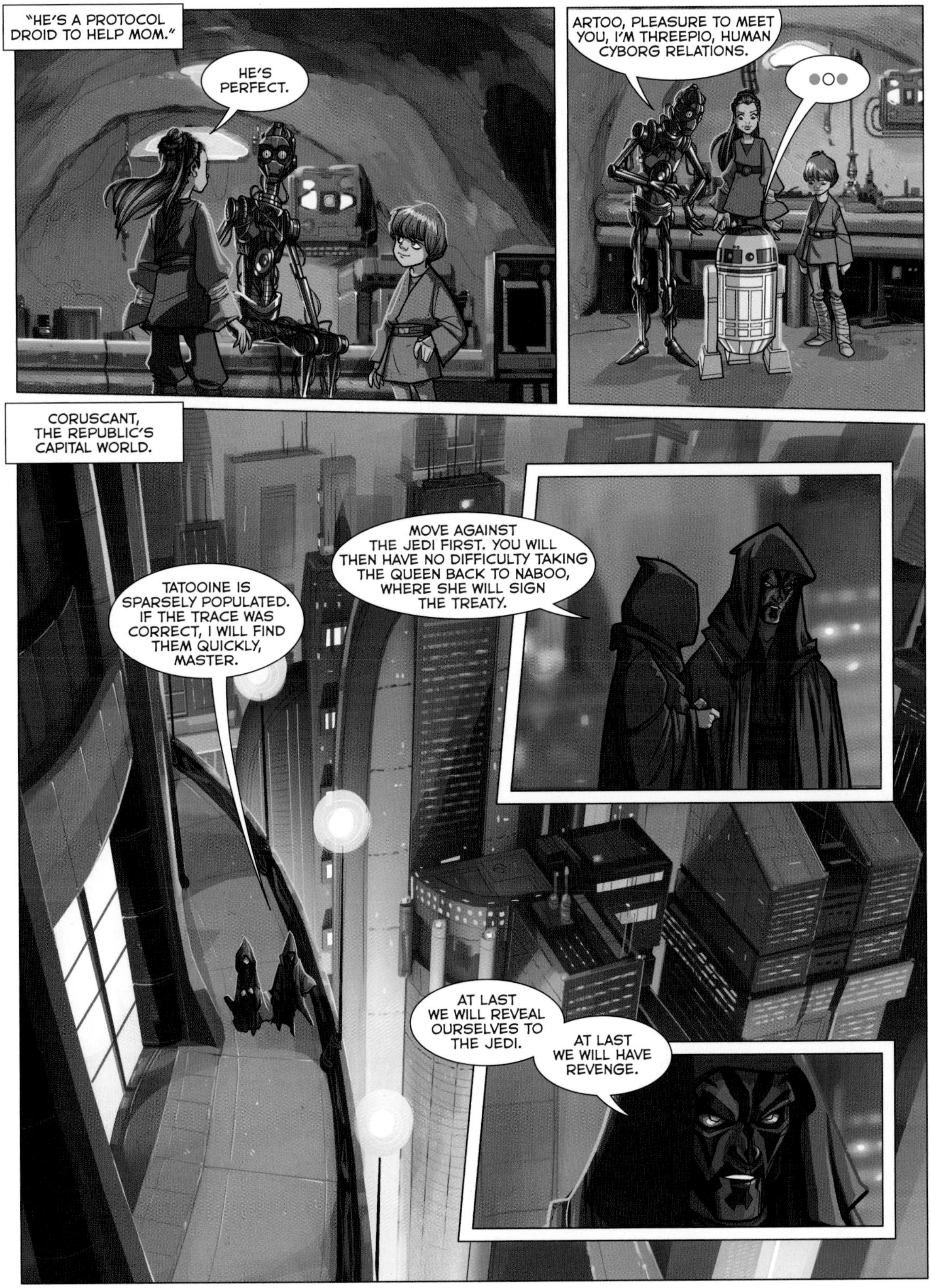
"HE'S A PROTOCOL DROID TO HELP MOM."
HE'S PERFECT.
ARTOO, PLEASURE TO MEET YOU, I'M THREEPIO, HUMAN CYBORG RELATIONS.
CORUSCANT, THE REPUBLIC'S CAPITAL WORLD.
TATOOINE IS SPARSELY POPULATED. IF THE TRACE WAS CORRECT, I WILL FIND THEM QUICKLY, MASTER.
MOVE AGAINST THE JEDI FIRST. YOU WILL THEN HAVE NO DIFFICULTY TAKING THE QUEEN BACK TO NABOO, WHERE SHE WILL SIGN THE TREATY.
AT LAST WE WILL REVEAL OURSELVES TO THE JEDI.
AT LAST WE WILL HAVE REVENGE.

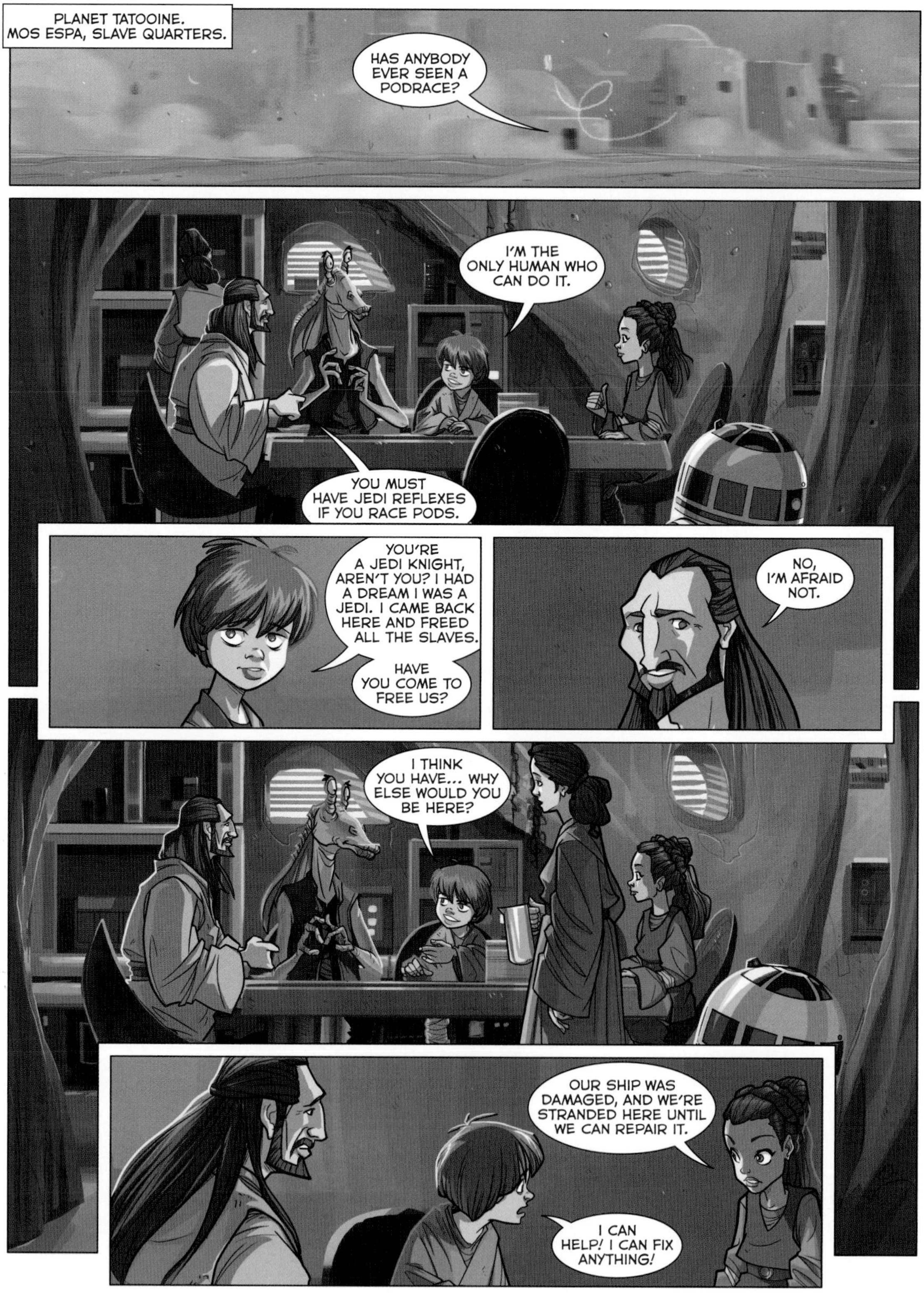
PLANET TATOOINE. MOS ESPA, SLAVE QUARTERS.
HAS ANYBODY EVER SEEN A PODRACE?
I'M THE ONLY HUMAN WHO CAN DO IT.
YOU MUST HAVE JEDI REFLEXES IF YOU RACE PODS.
YOU'RE A JEDI KNIGHT, AREN'T YOU? I HAD A DREAM I WAS A JEDI. I CAME BACK HERE AND FREED ALL THE SLAVES.
HAVE YOU COME TO FREE US?
NO, I'M AFRAID NOT.
I THINK YOU HAVE... WHY ELSE WOULD YOU BE HERE?
OUR SHIP WAS DAMAGED, AND WE'RE STRANDED HERE UNTIL WE CAN REPAIR IT.
I CAN HELP! I CAN FIX ANYTHING!

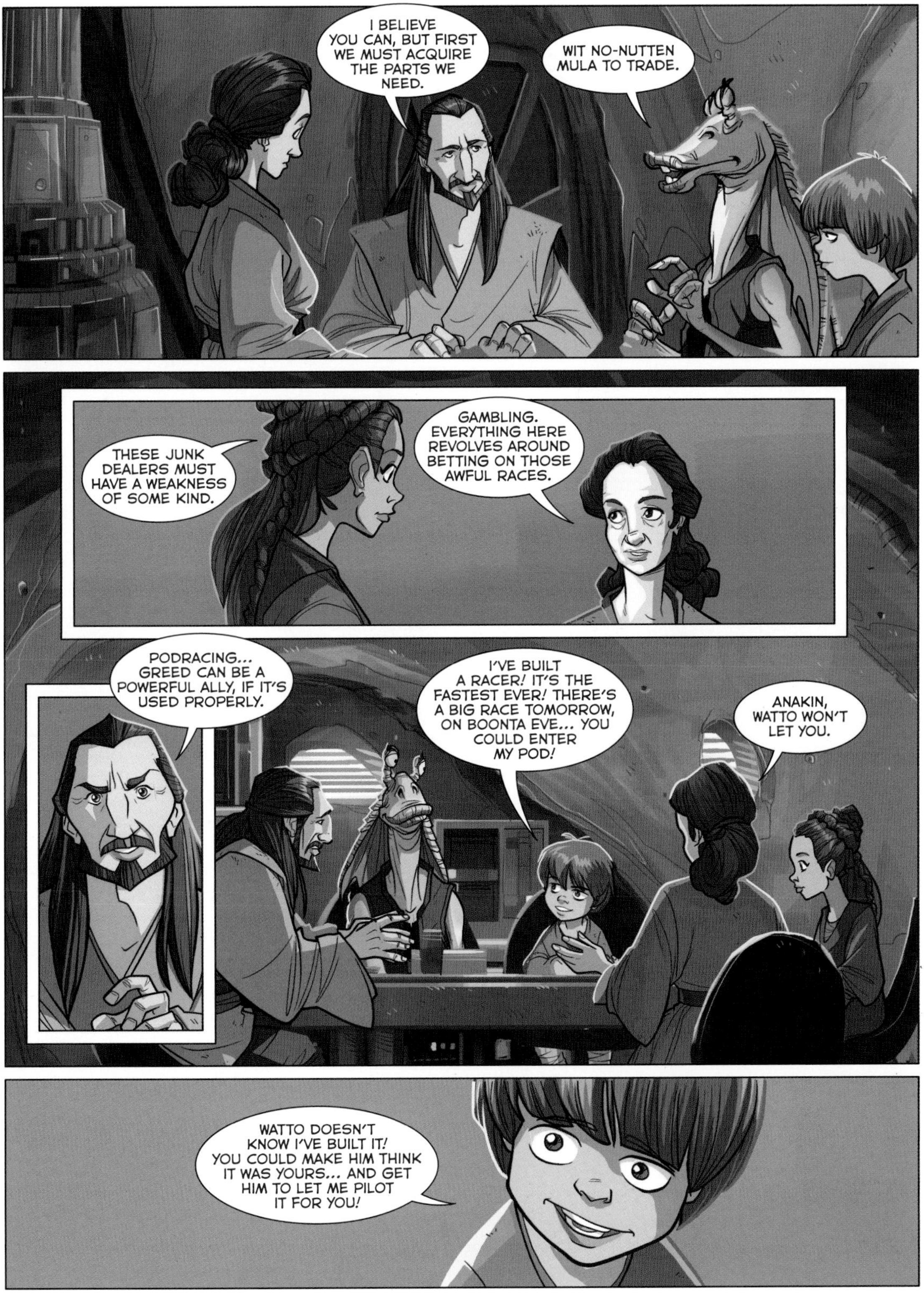
I BELIEVE YOU CAN, BUT FIRST WE MUST ACQUIRE THE PARTS WE NEED.
WIT NO-NUTTEN MULA TO TRADE.
THESE JUNK DEALERS MUST HAVE A WEAKNESS OF SOME KIND.
GAMBLING. EVERYTHING HERE REVOLVES AROUND BETTING ON THOSE AWFUL RACES.
PODRACING... GREED CAN BE A POWERFUL ALLY, IF IT'S USED PROPERLY.
I'VE BUILT A RACER! IT'S THE FASTEST EVER! THERE'S A BIG RACE TOMORROW, ON BOONTA EVE... YOU COULD ENTER MY POD!
ANAKIN, WATTO WON'T LET YOU.
WATTO DOESN'T KNOW I'VE BUILT IT! YOU COULD MAKE HIM THINK IT WAS YOURS... AND GET HIM TO LET ME PILOT IT FOR YOU!

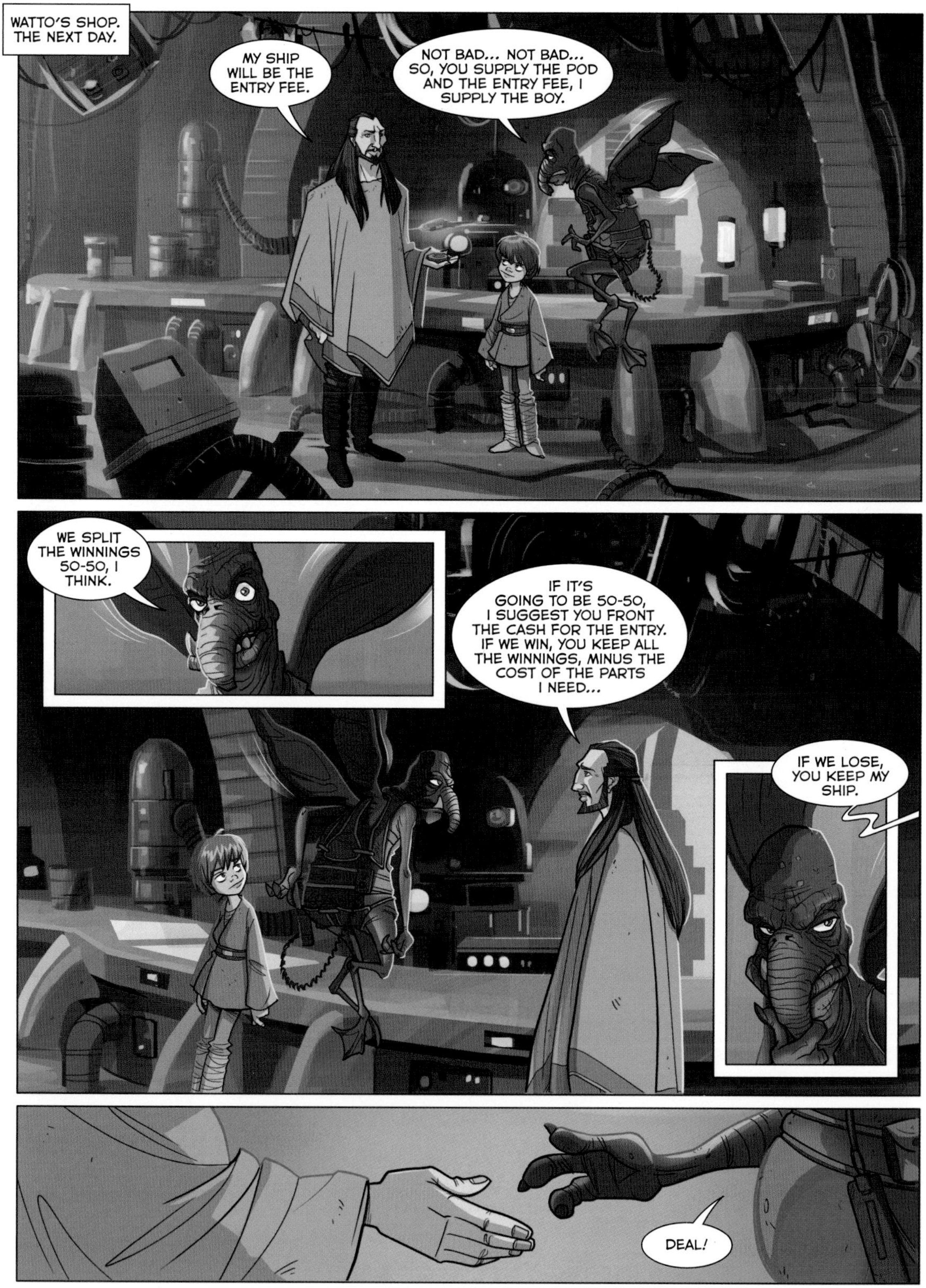
WATTO'S SHOP. THE NEXT DAY.
MY SHIP WILL BE THE ENTRY FEE.
NOT BAD... NOT BAD... SO, YOU SUPPLY THE POD AND THE ENTRY FEE, I SUPPLY THE BOY.
WE SPLIT THE WINNINGS 50-50, I THINK.
IF IT'S GOING TO BE 50-50, I SUGGEST YOU FRONT THE CASH FOR THE ENTRY. IF WE WIN, YOU KEEP ALL THE WINNINGS, MINUS THE COST OF THE PARTS I NEED...
IF WE LOSE, YOU KEEP MY SHIP.
DEAL!

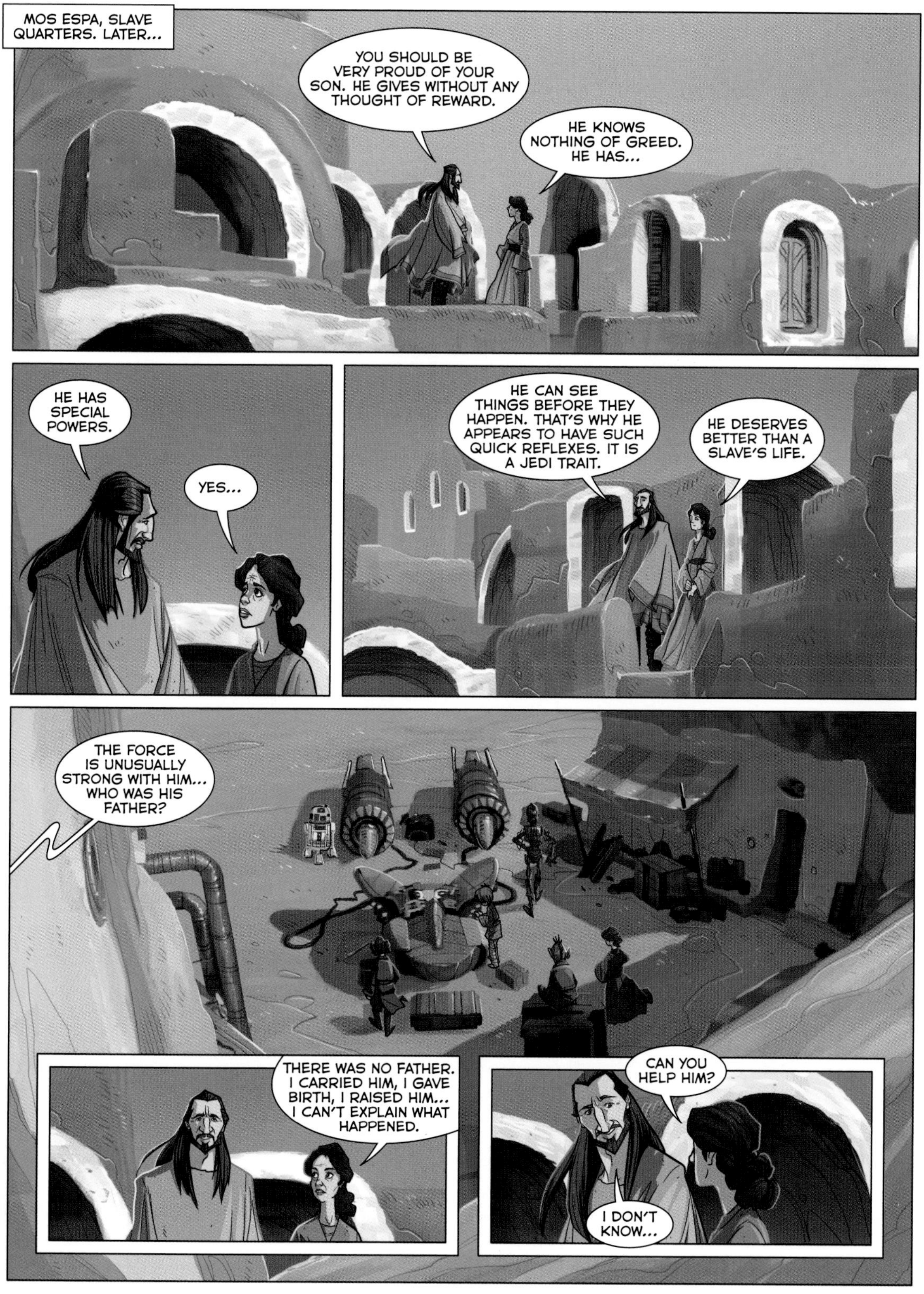
MOS ESPA, SLAVE QUARTERS. LATER...
YOU SHOULD BE VERY PROUD OF YOUR SON. HE GIVES WITHOUT ANY THOUGHT OF REWARD.
HE KNOWS NOTHING OF GREED. HE HAS...
HE HAS SPECIAL POWERS.
YES...
HE CAN SEE THINGS BEFORE THEY HAPPEN. THAT'S WHY HE APPEARS TO HAVE SUCH QUICK REFLEXES. IT IS A JEDI TRAIT.
HE DESERVES BETTER THAN A SLAVE'S LIFE.
THE FORCE IS UNUSUALLY STRONG WITH HIM... WHO WAS HIS FATHER?
THERE WAS NO FATHER. I CARRIED HIM, I GAVE BIRTH, I RAISED HIM... I CAN'T EXPLAIN WHAT HAPPENED.
CAN YOU HELP HIM?
I DON'T KNOW...

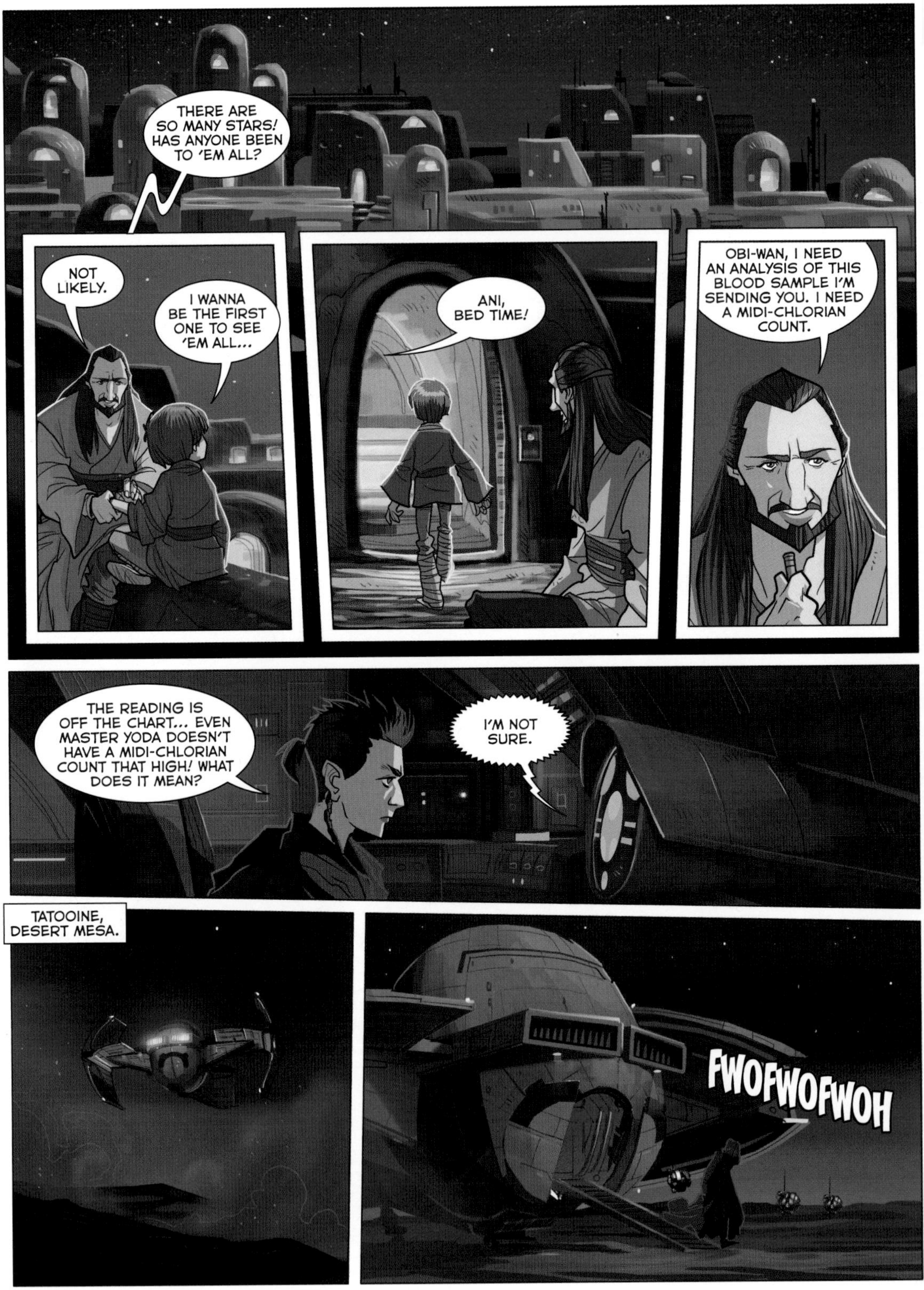
THERE ARE SO MANY STARS! HAS ANYONE BEEN TO 'EM ALL?
NOT LIKELY.
I WANNA BE THE FIRST ONE TO SEE 'EM ALL...
ANI, BED TIME!
OBI-WAN, I NEED AN ANALYSIS OF THIS BLOOD SAMPLE I'M SENDING YOU. I NEED A MIDI-CHLORIAN COUNT.
THE READING IS OFF THE CHART... EVEN MASTER YODA DOESN'T HAVE A MIDI-CHLORIAN COUNT THAT HIGH! WHAT DOES IT MEAN?
I'M NOT SURE.
TATOOINE, DESERT MESA.
FWOFWOFWOH

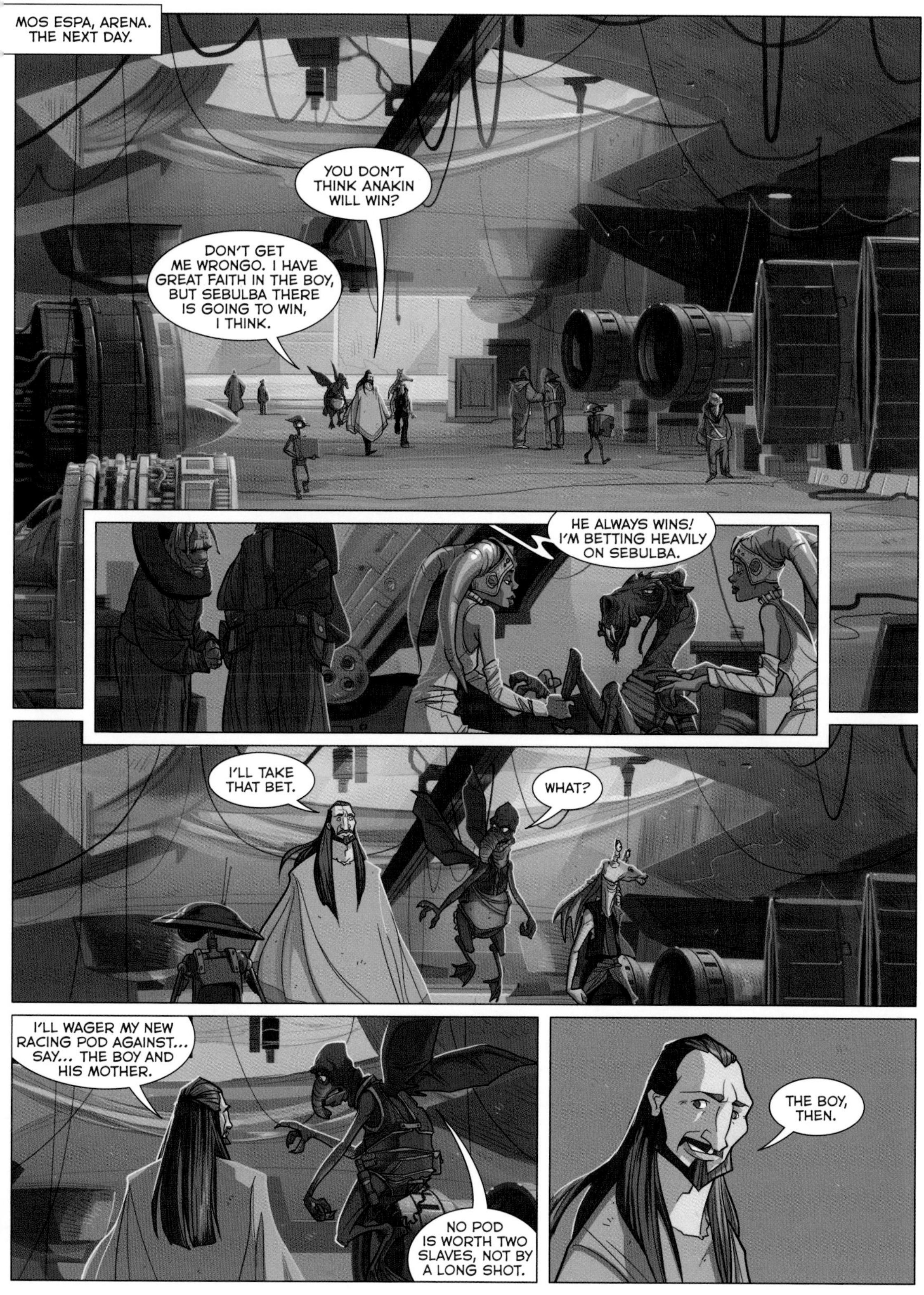
MOS ESPA, ARENA. THE NEXT DAY.
YOU DON'T THINK ANAKIN WILL WIN?
DON'T GET ME WRONGO. I HAVE GREAT FAITH IN THE BOY, BUT SEBULBA THERE IS GOING TO WIN, I THINK.
HE ALWAYS WINS! I'M BETTING HEAVILY ON SEBULBA.
I'LL TAKE THAT BET.
WHAT?
I'LL WAGER MY NEW RACING POD AGAINST... SAY... THE BOY AND HIS MOTHER.
NO POD IS WORTH TWO SLAVES, NOT BY A LONG SHOT.
THE BOY, THEN.

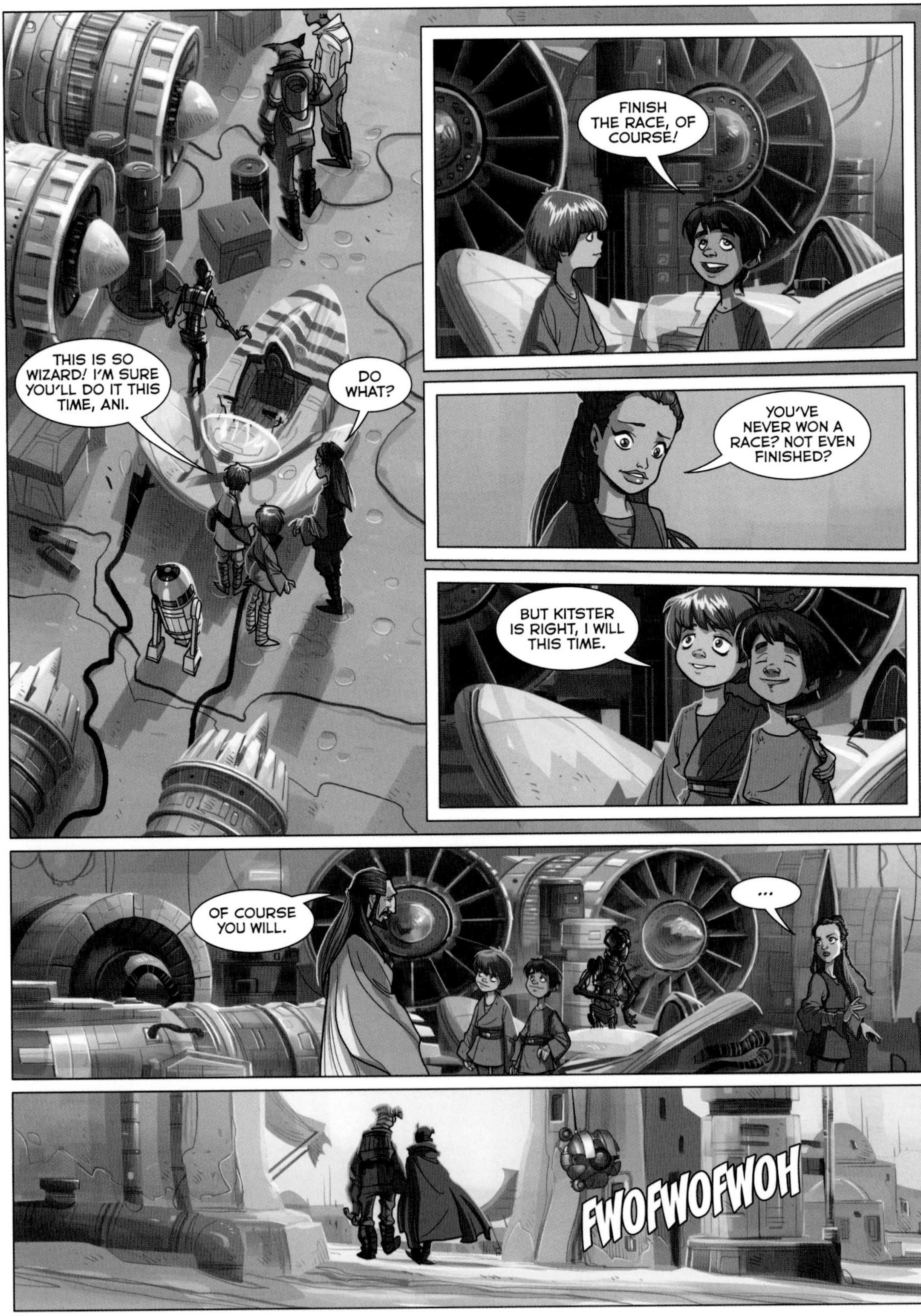
THIS IS SO WIZARD! I'M SURE YOU'LL DO IT THIS TIME, ANI.
DO WHAT?
FINISH THE RACE, OF COURSE!
YOU'VE NEVER WON A RACE? NOT EVEN FINISHED?
BUT KITSTER IS RIGHT, I WILL THIS TIME.
OF COURSE YOU WILL.
...
FWOFWOFWOH

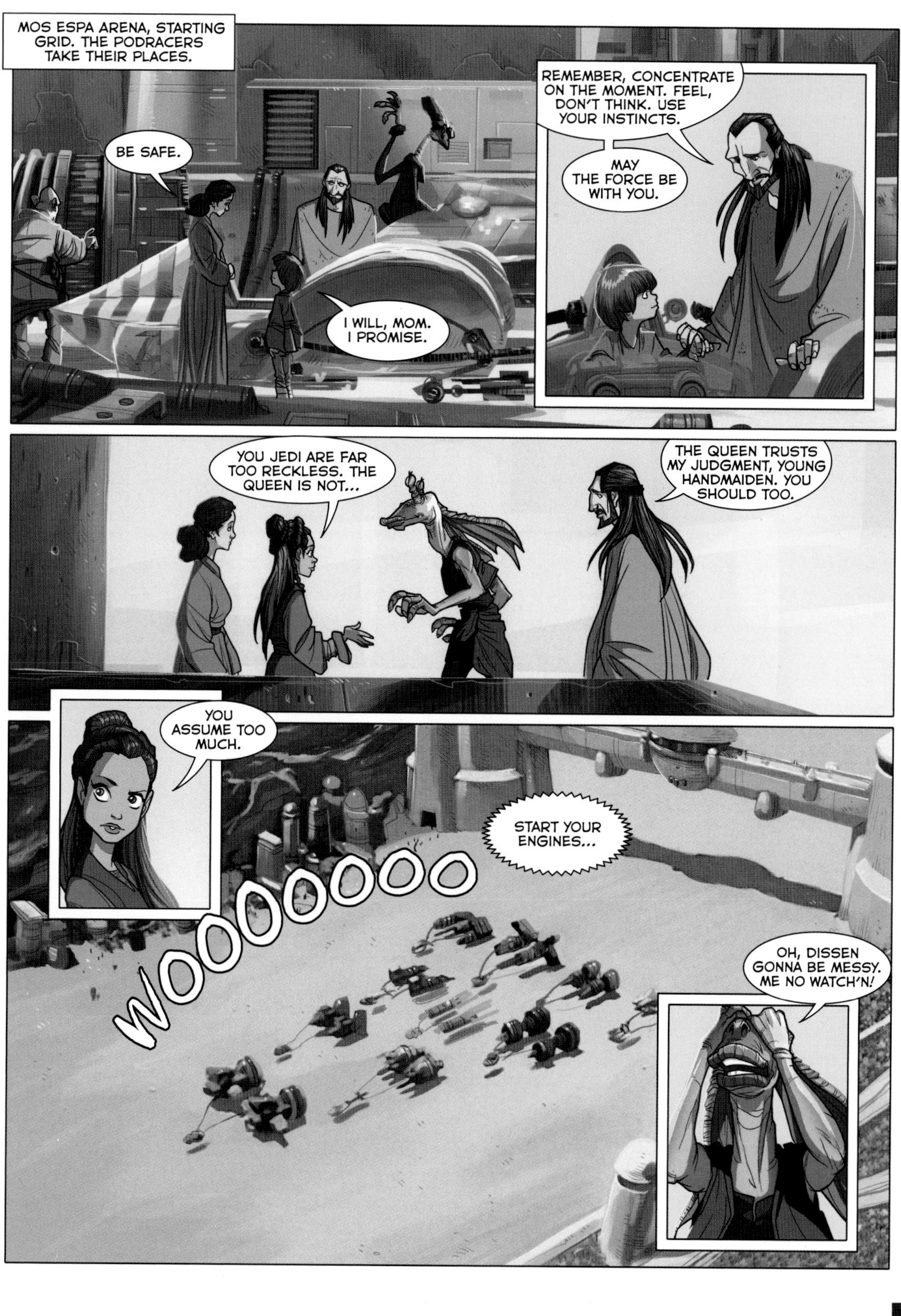
MOS ESPA ARENA, STARTING GRID. THE PODRACERS TAKE THEIR PLACES.
BE SAFE.
I WILL, MOM. I PROMISE.
REMEMBER, CONCENTRATE ON THE MOMENT. FEEL, DON'T THINK. USE YOUR INSTINCTS.
MAY THE FORCE BE WITH YOU.
YOU JEDI ARE FAR TOO RECKLESS. THE QUEEN IS NOT...
THE QUEEN TRUSTS MY JUDGMENT, YOUNG HANDMAIDEN. YOU SHOULD TOO.
YOU ASSUME TOO MUCH.
START YOUR ENGINES...
WOOOOOOOO
OH, DISSEN GONNA BE MESSY. ME NO WATCH'N!

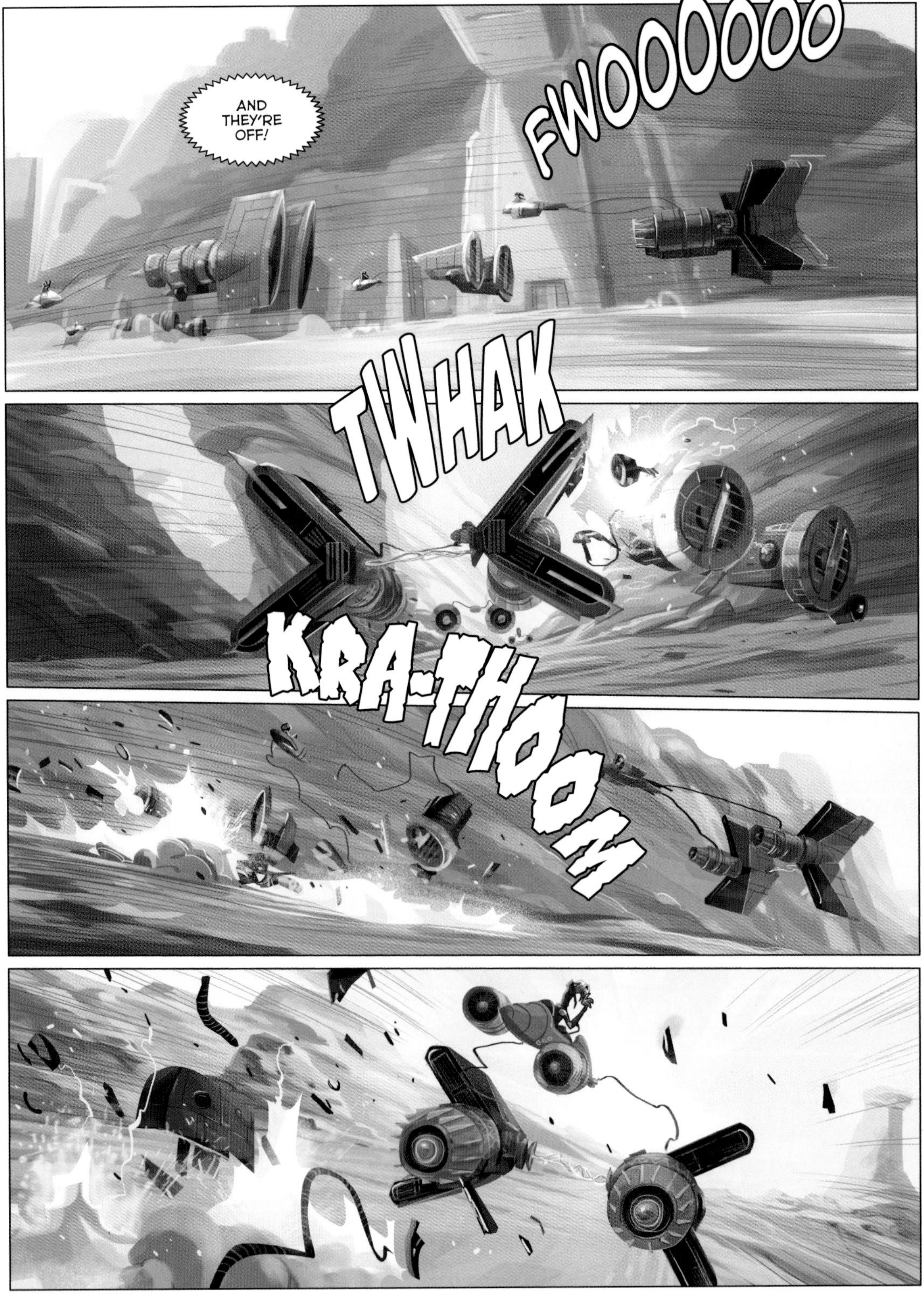
AND THEY'RE OFF!
FWOOOOOO
TWHAK
KRA-THOOM

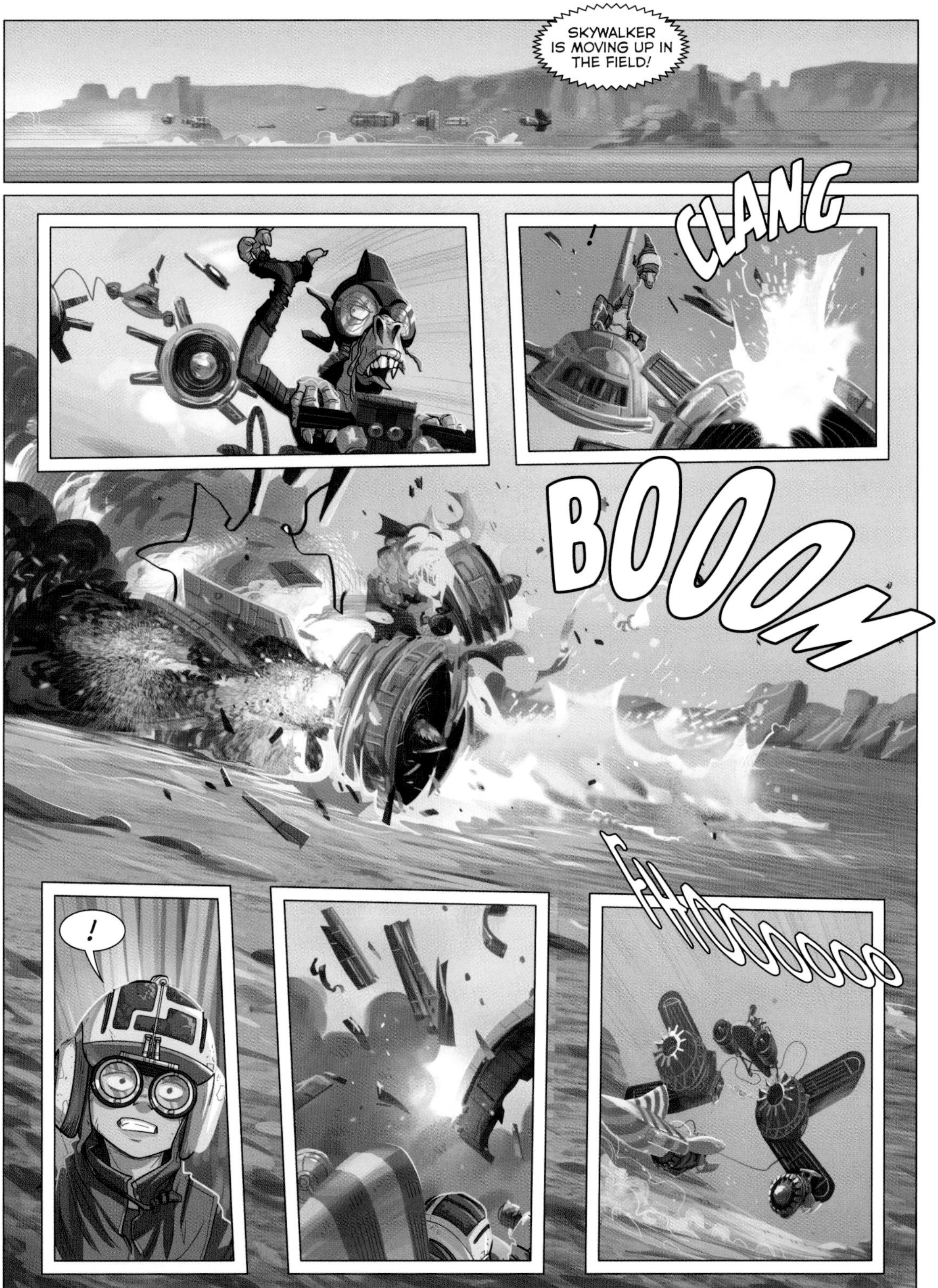
SKYWALKER IS MOVING UP IN THE FIELD!
CLANG
!
BOOOOM
!
FHOOOOOOO

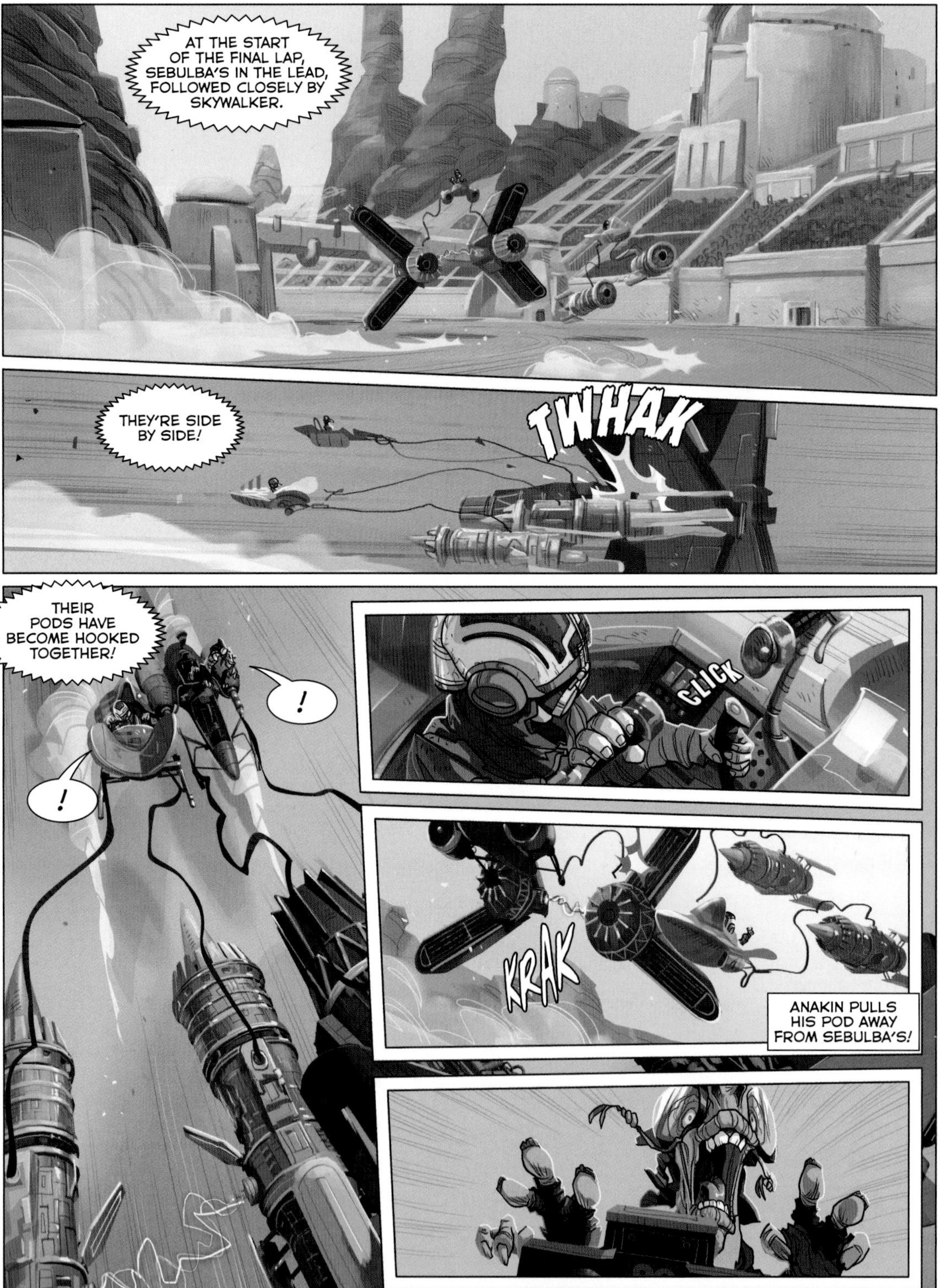
AT THE START OF THE FINAL LAP, SEBULBA'S IN THE LEAD, FOLLOWED CLOSELY BY SKYWALKER.
THEY'RE SIDE BY SIDE!
TWHAK
THEIR PODS HAVE BECOME HOOKED TOGETHER!
!
!
CLICK
KRAK
ANAKIN PULLS HIS POD AWAY FROM SEBULBA'S!

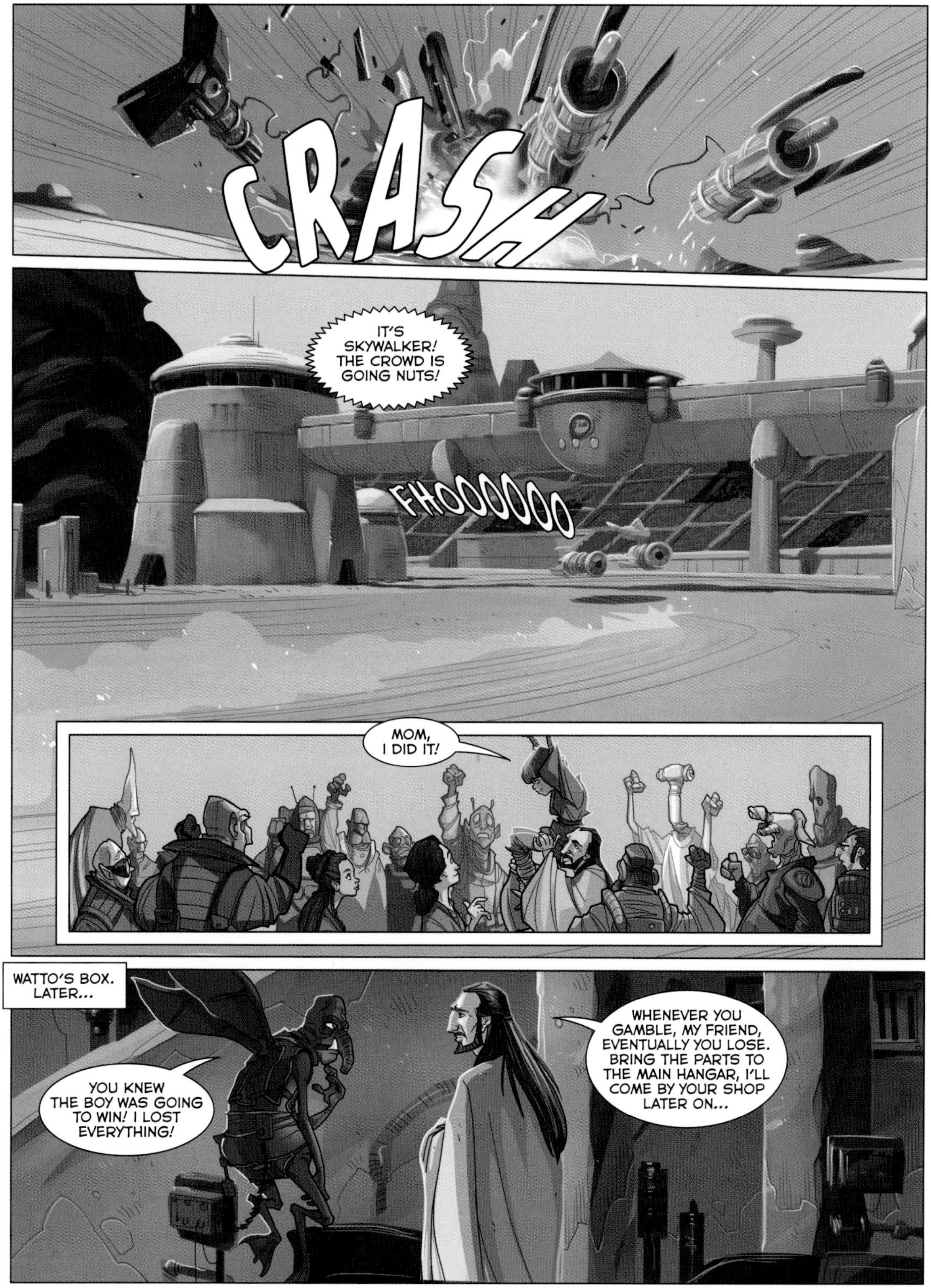
CRASH
IT'S SKYWALKER! THE CROWD IS GOING NUTS!
FHOOOOOO
MOM, I DID IT!
WATTO'S BOX. LATER...
YOU KNEW THE BOY WAS GOING TO WIN! I LOST EVERYTHING!
WHENEVER YOU GAMBLE, MY FRIEND, EVENTUALLY YOU LOSE. BRING THE PARTS TO THE MAIN HANGAR, I'LL COME BY YOUR SHOP LATER ON...

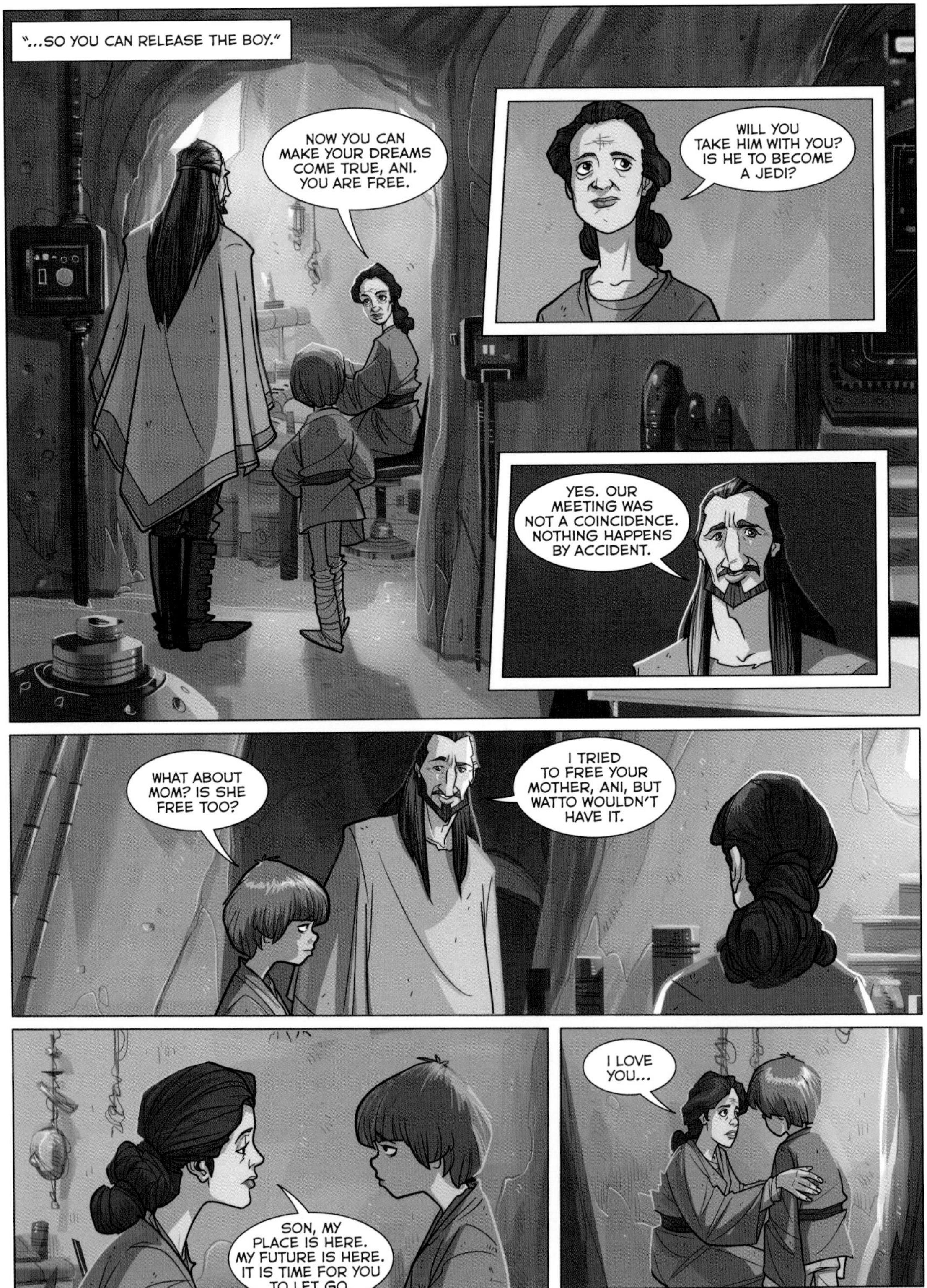
"...SO YOU CAN RELEASE THE BOY."
NOW YOU CAN MAKE YOUR DREAMS COME TRUE, ANI. YOU ARE FREE.
WILL YOU TAKE HIM WITH YOU? IS HE TO BECOME A JEDI?
YES. OUR MEETING WAS NOT A COINCIDENCE. NOTHING HAPPENS BY ACCIDENT.
WHAT ABOUT MOM? IS SHE FREE TOO?
I TRIED TO FREE YOUR MOTHER, ANI, BUT WATTO WOULDN'T HAVE IT.
SON, MY PLACE IS HERE. MY FUTURE IS HERE. IT IS TIME FOR YOU TO LET GO.
I LOVE YOU...

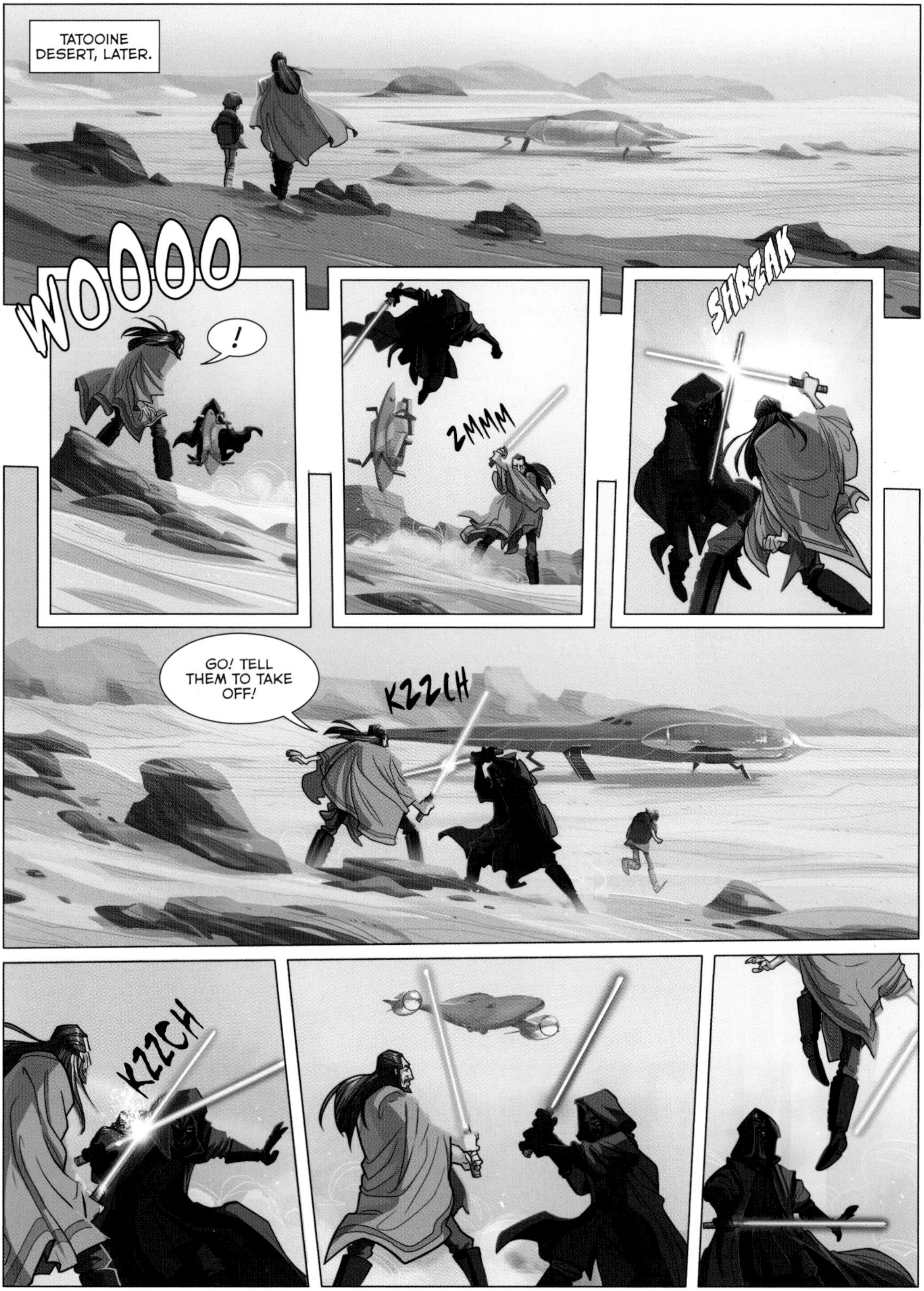
TATOOINE DESERT, LATER.
WOOOO
!
ZMMM
SHRZAK
GO! TELL THEM TO TAKE OFF!
KZZCH
KZZCH

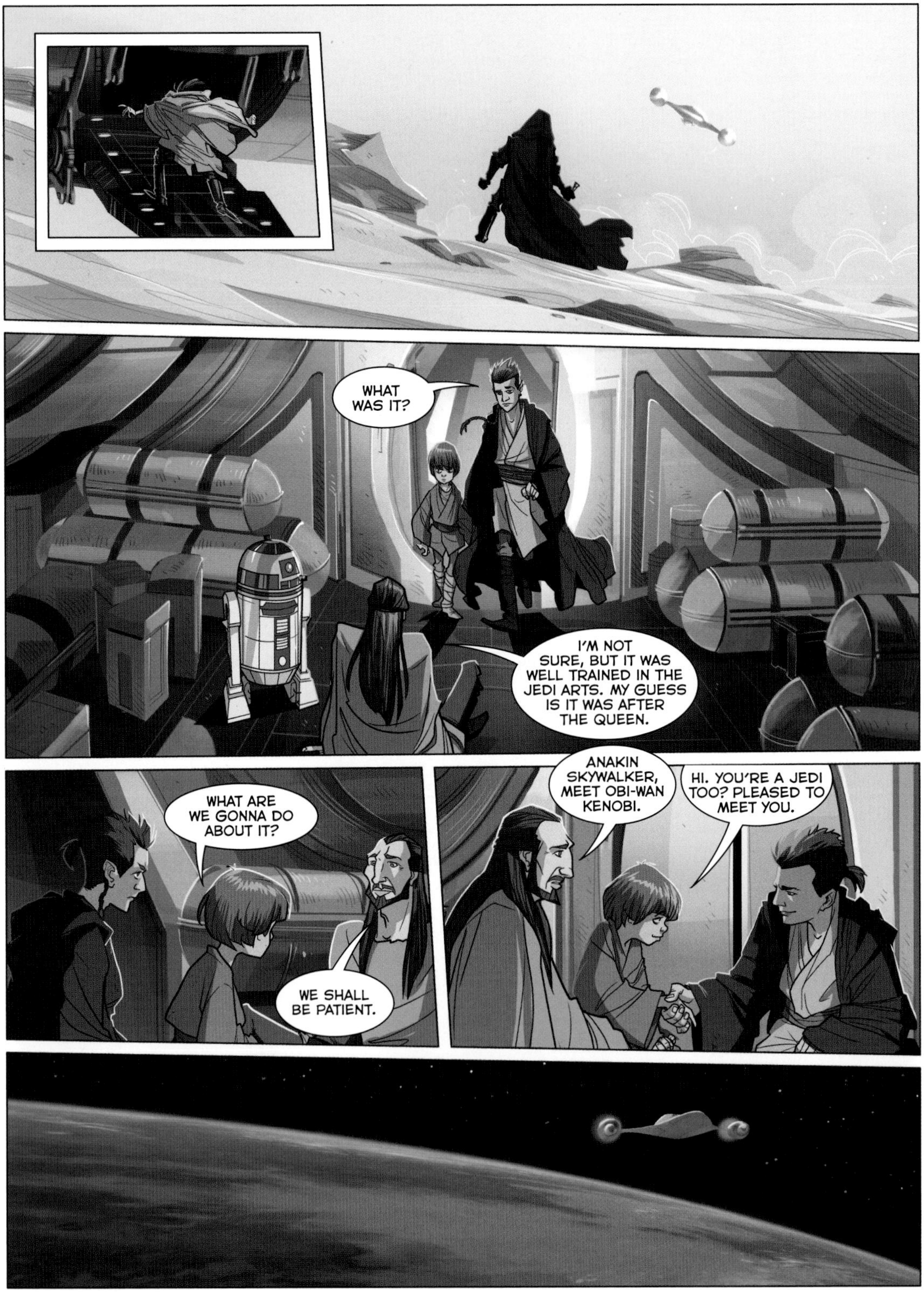
WHAT WAS IT?
I'M NOT SURE, BUT IT WAS WELL TRAINED IN THE JEDI ARTS. MY GUESS IS IT WAS AFTER THE QUEEN.
WHAT ARE WE GONNA DO ABOUT IT?
WE SHALL BE PATIENT.
ANAKIN SKYWALKER, MEET OBI-WAN KENOBI.
HI. YOU'RE A JEDI TOO? PLEASED TO MEET YOU.

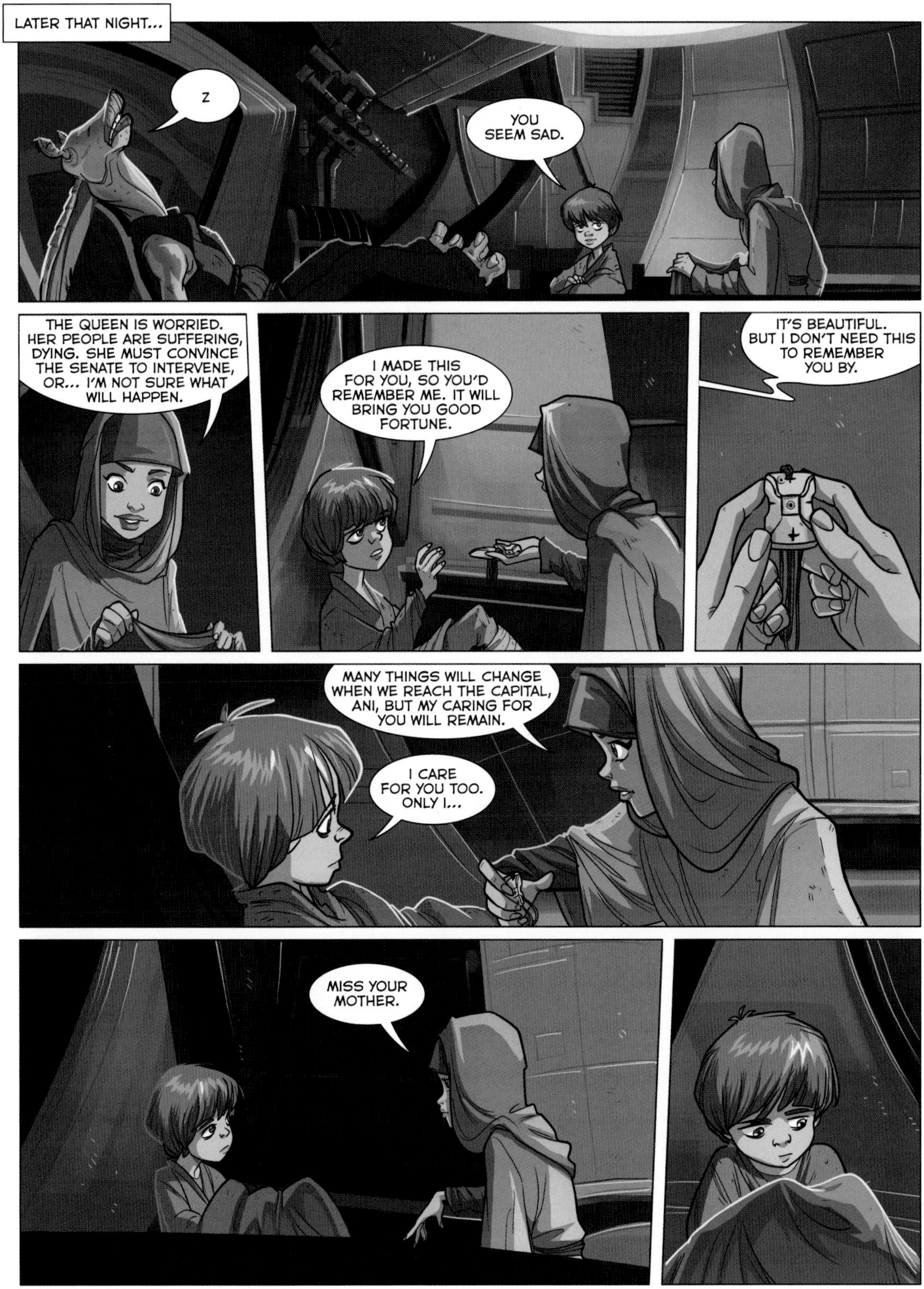
LATER THAT NIGHT...
Z
YOU SEEM SAD.
THE QUEEN IS WORRIED. HER PEOPLE ARE SUFFERING, DYING. SHE MUST CONVINCE THE SENATE TO INTERVENE, OR... I'M NOT SURE WHAT WILL HAPPEN.
I MADE THIS FOR YOU, SO YOU'D REMEMBER ME. IT WILL BRING YOU GOOD FORTUNE.
IT'S BEAUTIFUL. BUT I DON'T NEED THIS TO REMEMBER YOU BY.
MANY THINGS WILL CHANGE WHEN WE REACH THE CAPITAL, ANI, BUT MY CARING FOR YOU WILL REMAIN.
I CARE FOR YOU TOO. ONLY I...
MISS YOUR MOTHER.

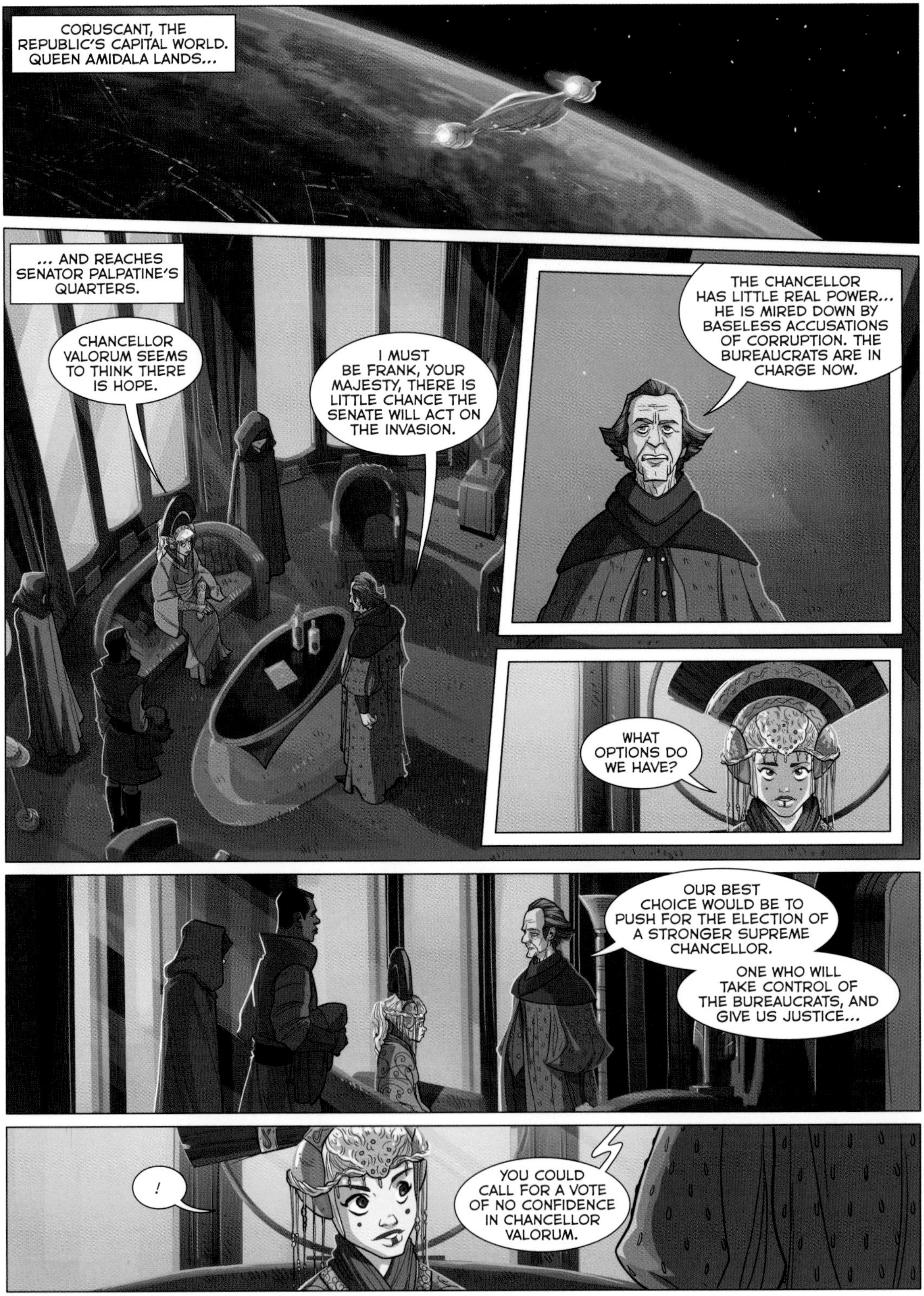
CORUSCANT, THE REPUBLIC'S CAPITAL WORLD. QUEEN AMIDALA LANDS...
... AND REACHES SENATOR PALPATINE'S QUARTERS.
CHANCELLOR VALORUM SEEMS TO THINK THERE IS HOPE.
I MUST BE FRANK, YOUR MAJESTY, THERE IS LITTLE CHANCE THE SENATE WILL ACT ON THE INVASION.
THE CHANCELLOR HAS LITTLE REAL POWER... HE IS MIRED DOWN BY BASELESS ACCUSATIONS OF CORRUPTION. THE BUREAUCRATS ARE IN CHARGE NOW.
WHAT OPTIONS DO WE HAVE?
OUR BEST CHOICE WOULD BE TO PUSH FOR THE ELECTION OF A STRONGER SUPREME CHANCELLOR.
ONE WHO WILL TAKE CONTROL OF THE BUREAUCRATS, AND GIVE US JUSTICE...
!
YOU COULD CALL FOR A VOTE OF NO CONFIDENCE IN CHANCELLOR VALORUM.

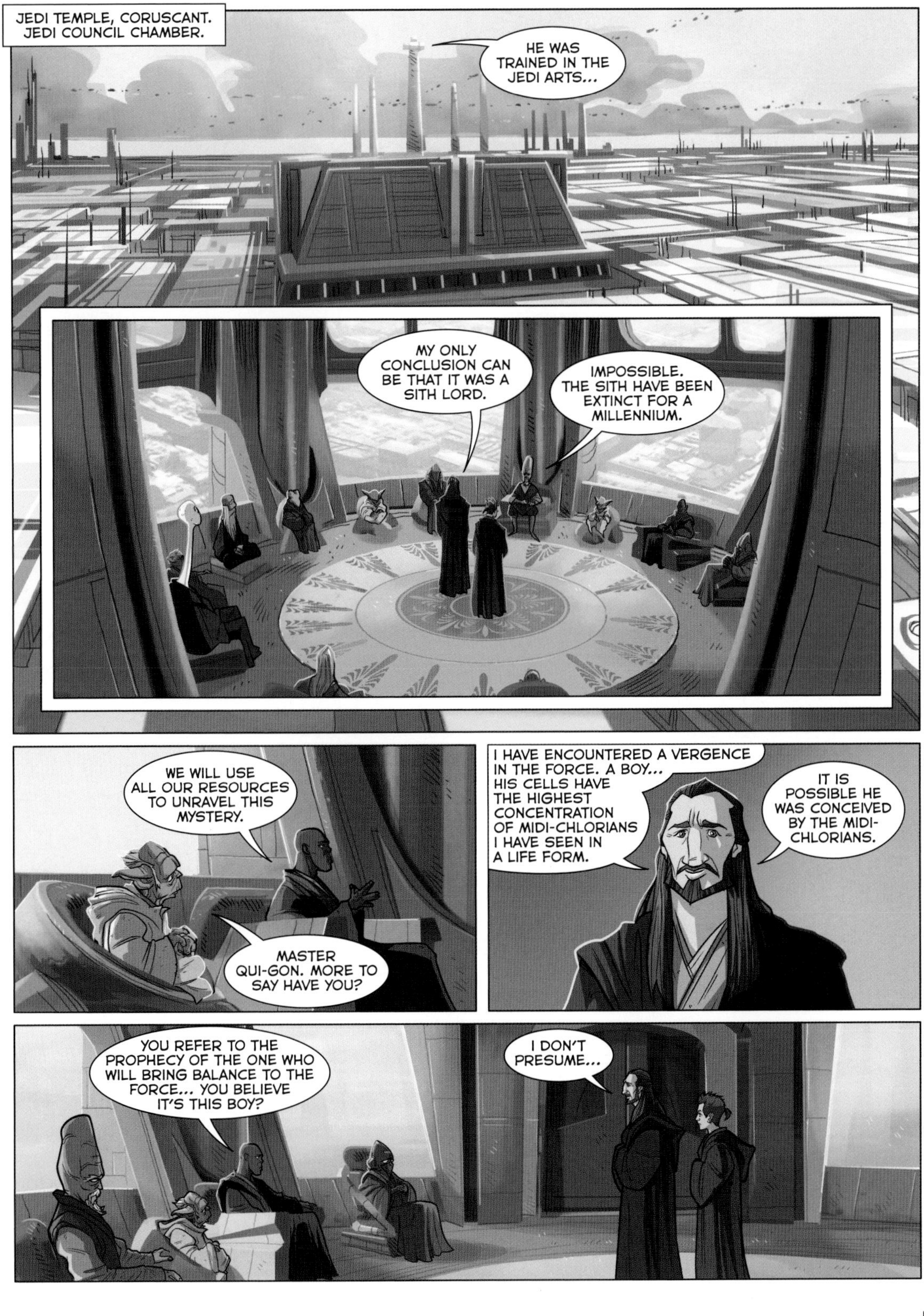
JEDI TEMPLE, CORUSCANT. JEDI COUNCIL CHAMBER.
HE WAS TRAINED IN THE JEDI ARTS...
MY ONLY CONCLUSION CAN BE THAT IT WAS A SITH LORD.
IMPOSSIBLE. THE SITH HAVE BEEN EXTINCT FOR A MILLENNIUM.
WE WILL USE ALL OUR RESOURCES TO UNRAVEL THIS MYSTERY.
MASTER QUI-GON. MORE TO SAY HAVE YOU?
I HAVE ENCOUNTERED A VERGENCE IN THE FORCE. A BOY... HIS CELLS HAVE THE HIGHEST CONCENTRATION OF MIDI-CHLORIANS I HAVE SEEN IN A LIFE FORM.
IT IS POSSIBLE HE WAS CONCEIVED BY THE MIDI-CHLORIANS.
YOU REFER TO THE PROPHECY OF THE ONE WHO WILL BRING BALANCE TO THE FORCE... YOU BELIEVE IT'S THIS BOY?
I DON'T PRESUME...

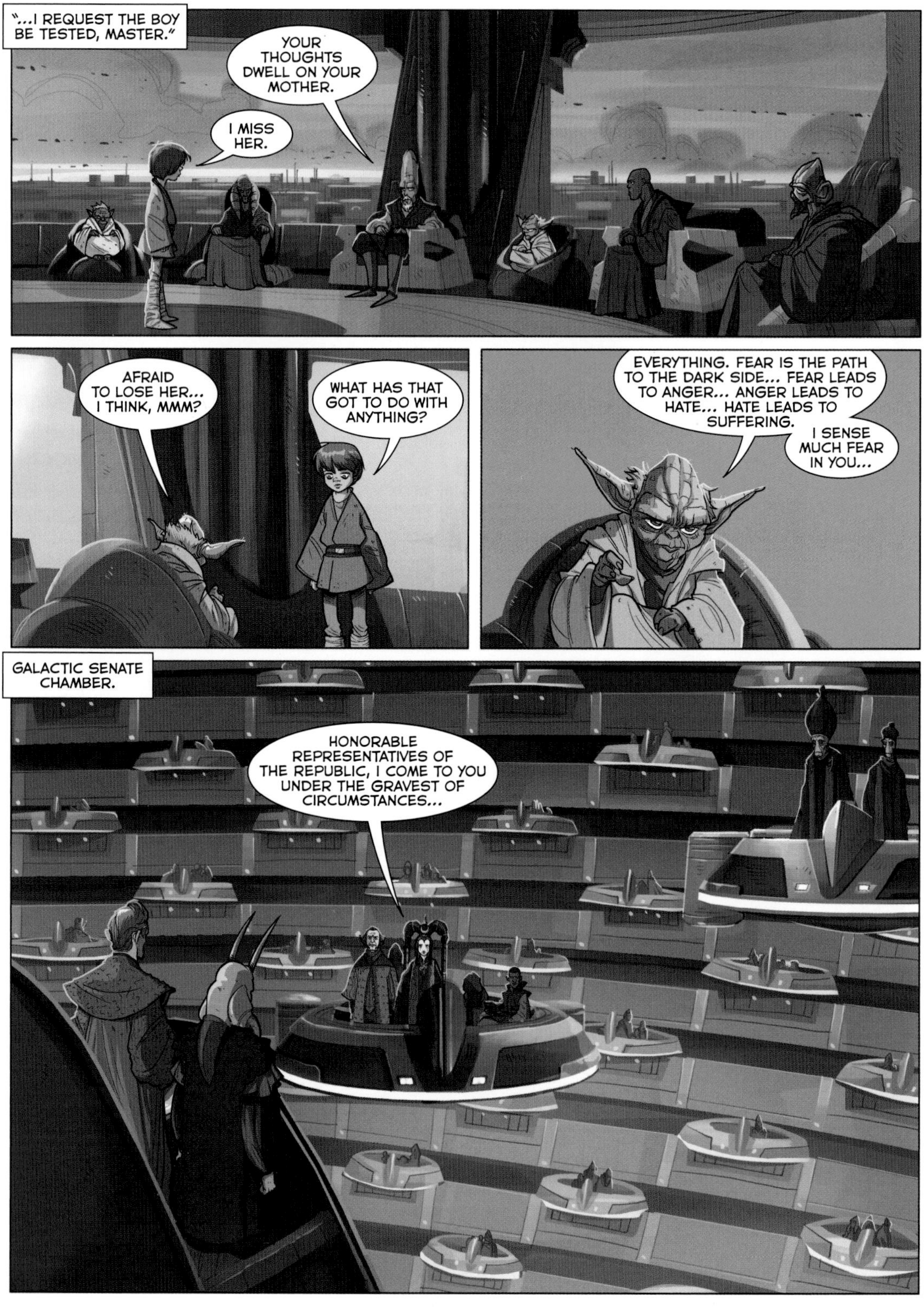
"...I REQUEST THE BOY BE TESTED, MASTER."
YOUR THOUGHTS DWELL ON YOUR MOTHER.
I MISS HER.
AFRAID TO LOSE HER... I THINK, MMM?
WHAT HAS THAT GOT TO DO WITH ANYTHING?
EVERYTHING. FEAR IS THE PATH TO THE DARK SIDE... FEAR LEADS TO ANGER... ANGER LEADS TO HATE... HATE LEADS TO SUFFERING.
I SENSE MUCH FEAR IN YOU...
GALACTIC SENATE CHAMBER.
HONORABLE REPRESENTATIVES OF THE REPUBLIC, I COME TO YOU UNDER THE GRAVEST OF CIRCUMSTANCES...

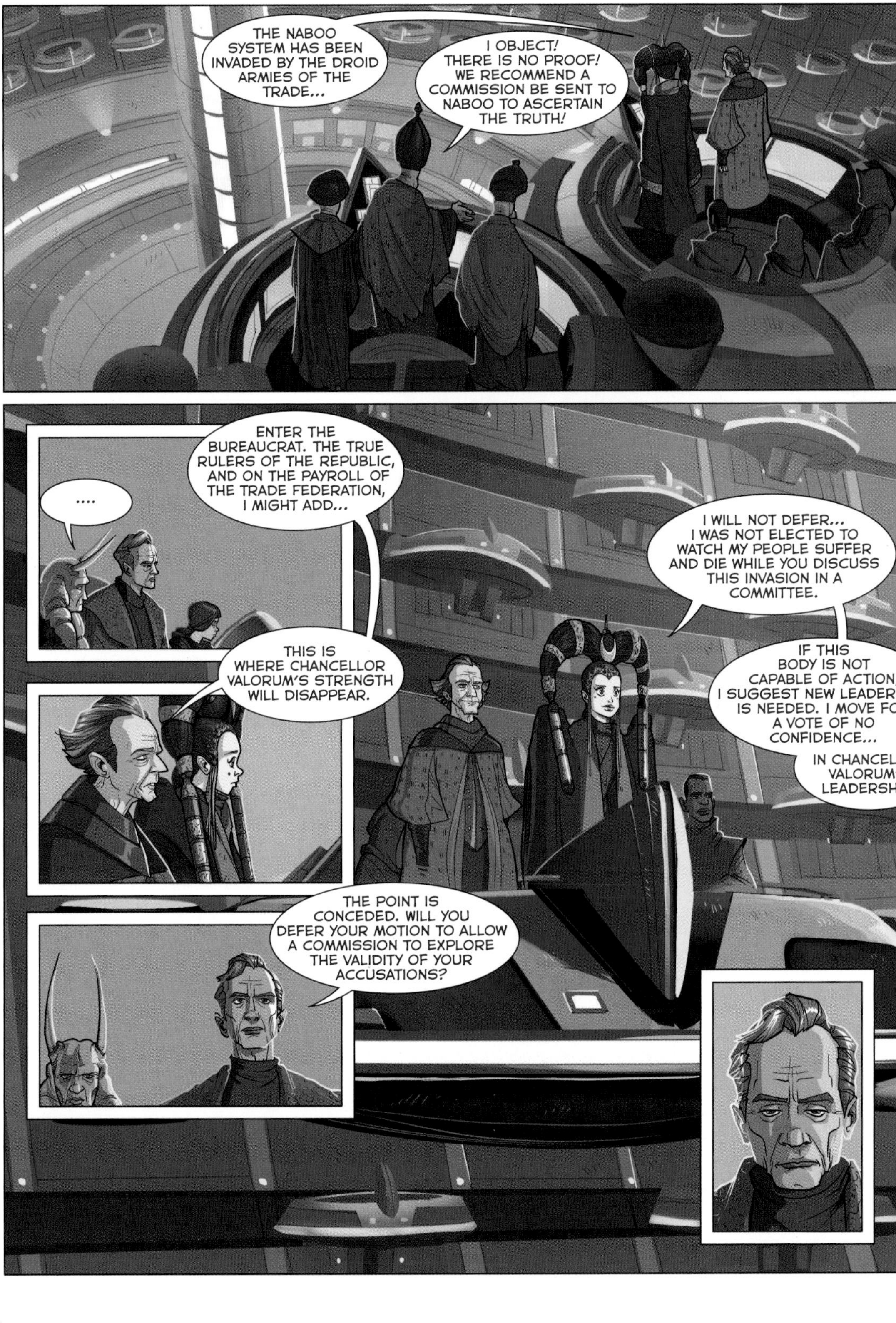

THE NABOO SYSTEM HAS BEEN INVADED BY THE DROID ARMIES OF THE TRADE...
I OBJECT! THERE IS NO PROOF! WE RECOMMEND A COMMISSION BE SENT TO NABOO TO ASCERTAIN THE TRUTH!
ENTER THE BUREAUCRAT. THE TRUE RULERS OF THE REPUBLIC, AND ON THE PAYROLL OF THE TRADE FEDERATION, I MIGHT ADD...
....
THIS IS WHERE CHANCELLOR VALORUM'S STRENGTH WILL DISAPPEAR.
THE POINT IS CONCEDED. WILL YOU DEFER YOUR MOTION TO ALLOW A COMMISSION TO EXPLORE THE VALIDITY OF YOUR ACCUSATIONS?
I WILL NOT DEFER... I WAS NOT ELECTED TO WATCH MY PEOPLE SUFFER AND DIE WHILE YOU DISCUSS THIS INVASION IN A COMMITTEE.
IF THIS BODY IS NOT CAPABLE OF ACTION, I SUGGEST NEW LEADERSHIP IS NEEDED. I MOVE FOR A VOTE OF NO CONFIDENCE...
IN CHANCELLOR VALORUM'S LEADERSHIP!

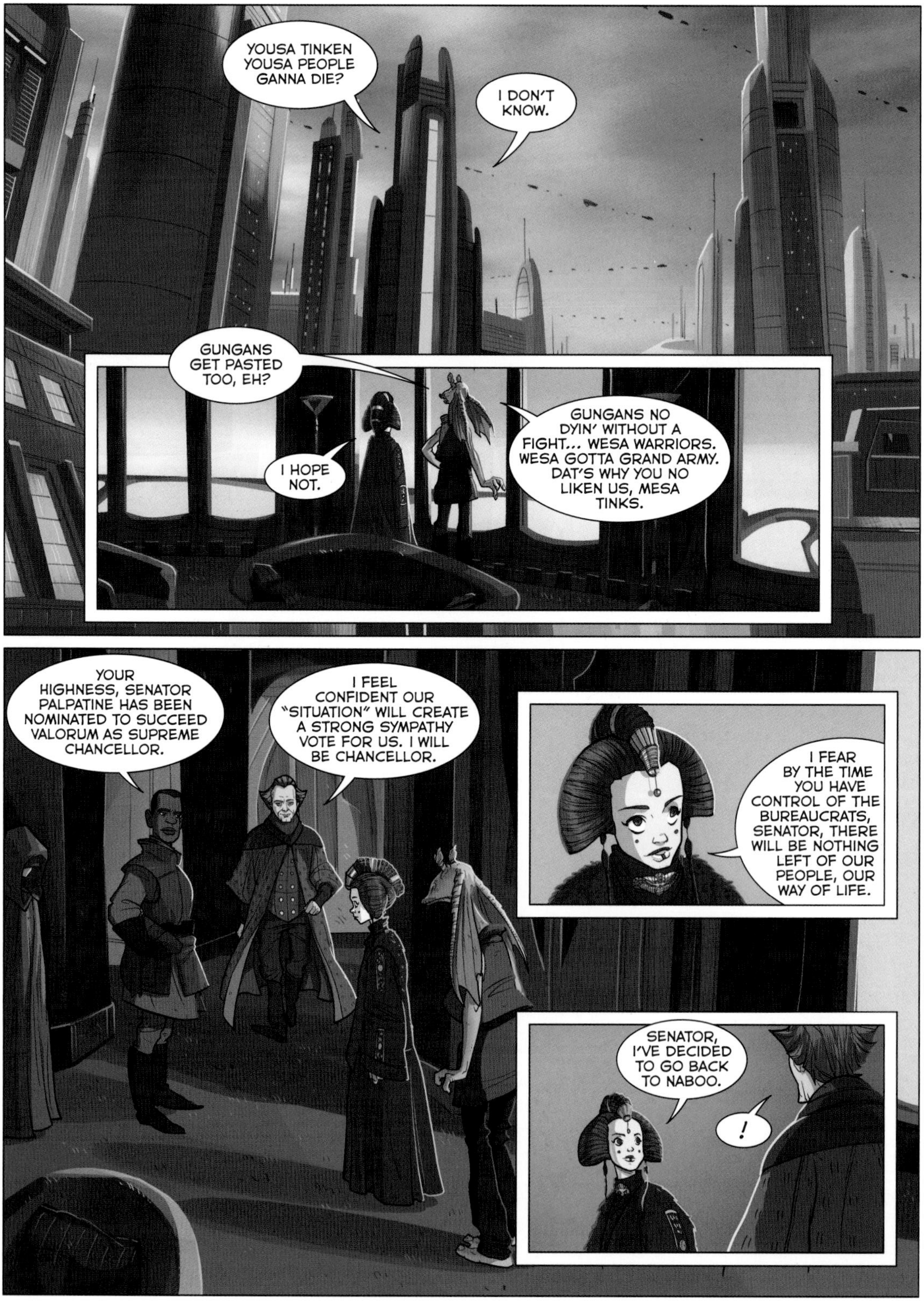

YOUSA TINKEN YOUSA PEOPLE GANNA DIE?
I DON'T KNOW.
GUNGANS GET PASTED TOO, EH?
I HOPE NOT.
GUNGANS NO DYIN' WITHOUT A FIGHT... WESA WARRIORS. WESA GOTTA GRAND ARMY. DAT'S WHY YOU NO LIKEN US, MESA TINKS.
YOUR HIGHNESS, SENATOR PALPATINE HAS BEEN NOMINATED TO SUCCEED VALORUM AS SUPREME CHANCELLOR.
I FEEL CONFIDENT OUR "SITUATION" WILL CREATE A STRONG SYMPATHY VOTE FOR US. I WILL BE CHANCELLOR.
I FEAR BY THE TIME YOU HAVE CONTROL OF THE BUREAUCRATS, SENATOR, THERE WILL BE NOTHING LEFT OF OUR PEOPLE, OUR WAY OF LIFE.
SENATOR, I'VE DECIDED TO GO BACK TO NABOO.
!

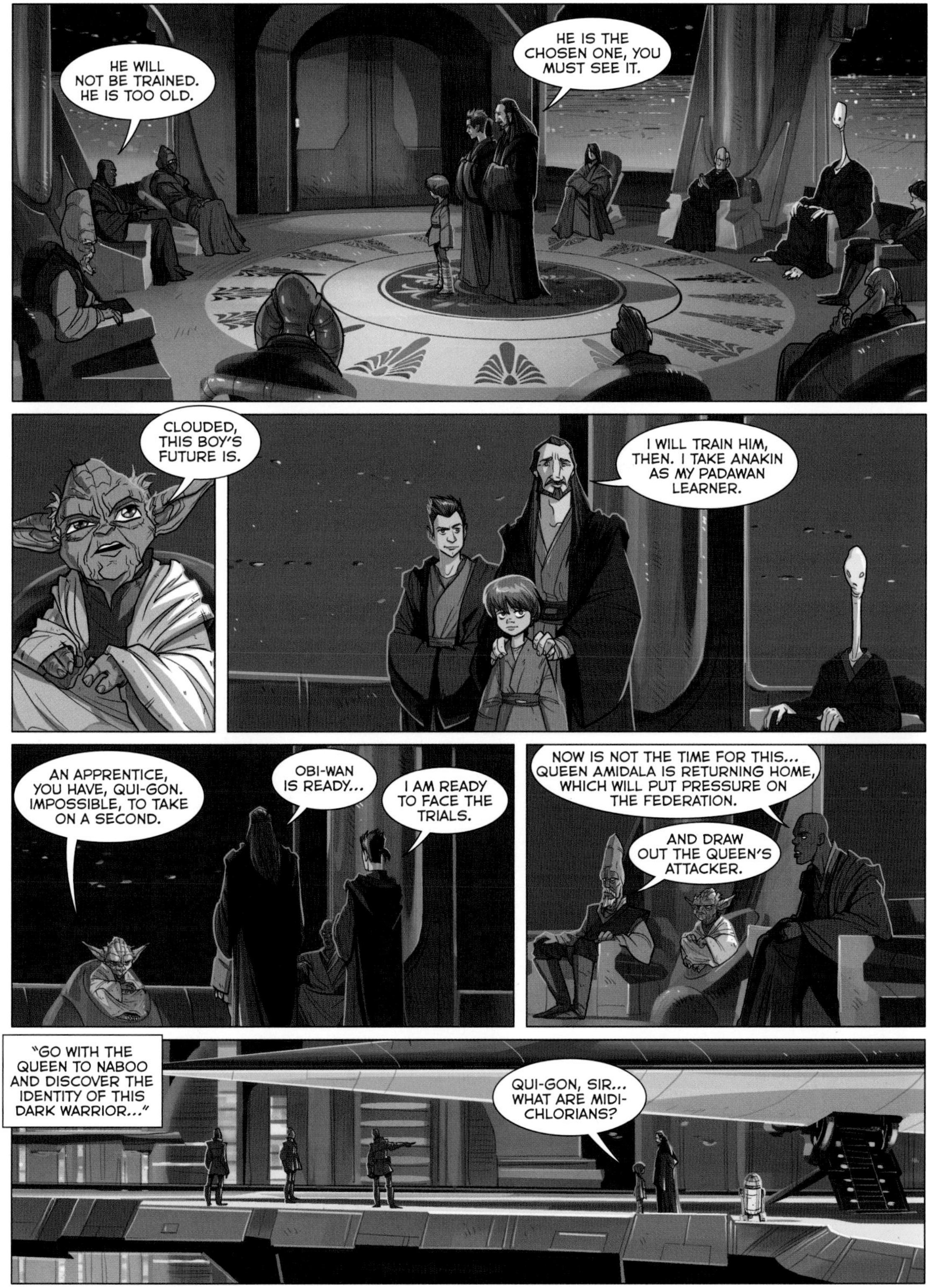
HE WILL NOT BE TRAINED. HE IS TOO OLD.
HE IS THE CHOSEN ONE, YOU MUST SEE IT.
CLOUDED, THIS BOY'S FUTURE IS.
I WILL TRAIN HIM, THEN. I TAKE ANAKIN AS MY PADAWAN LEARNER.
AN APPRENTICE, YOU HAVE, QUI-GON. IMPOSSIBLE, TO TAKE ON A SECOND.
OBI-WAN IS READY...
I AM READY TO FACE THE TRIALS.
NOW IS NOT THE TIME FOR THIS... QUEEN AMIDALA IS RETURNING HOME, WHICH WILL PUT PRESSURE ON THE FEDERATION.
AND DRAW OUT THE QUEEN'S ATTACKER.
"GO WITH THE QUEEN TO NABOO AND DISCOVER THE IDENTITY OF THIS DARK WARRIOR..."
QUI-GON, SIR... WHAT ARE MIDI-CHLORIANS?

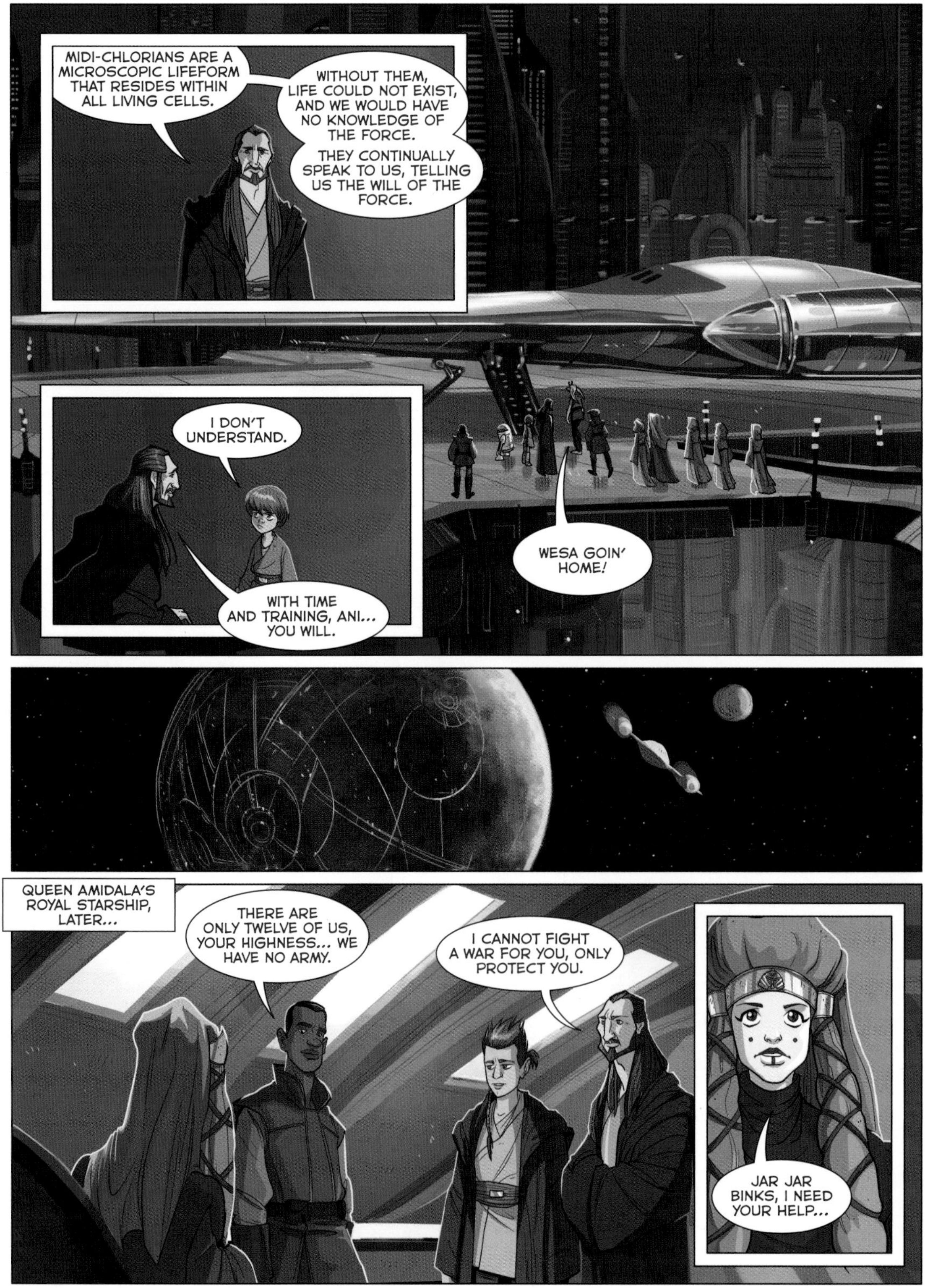
MIDI-CHLORIANS ARE A MICROSCOPIC LIFEFORM THAT RESIDES WITHIN ALL LIVING CELLS.
WITHOUT THEM, LIFE COULD NOT EXIST, AND WE WOULD HAVE NO KNOWLEDGE OF THE FORCE.
THEY CONTINUALLY SPEAK TO US, TELLING US THE WILL OF THE FORCE.
I DON'T UNDERSTAND.
WITH TIME AND TRAINING, ANI... YOU WILL.
WESA GOIN' HOME!
QUEEN AMIDALA'S ROYAL STARSHIP, LATER...
THERE ARE ONLY TWELVE OF US, YOUR HIGHNESS... WE HAVE NO ARMY.
I CANNOT FIGHT A WAR FOR YOU, ONLY PROTECT YOU.
JAR JAR BINKS, I NEED YOUR HELP...

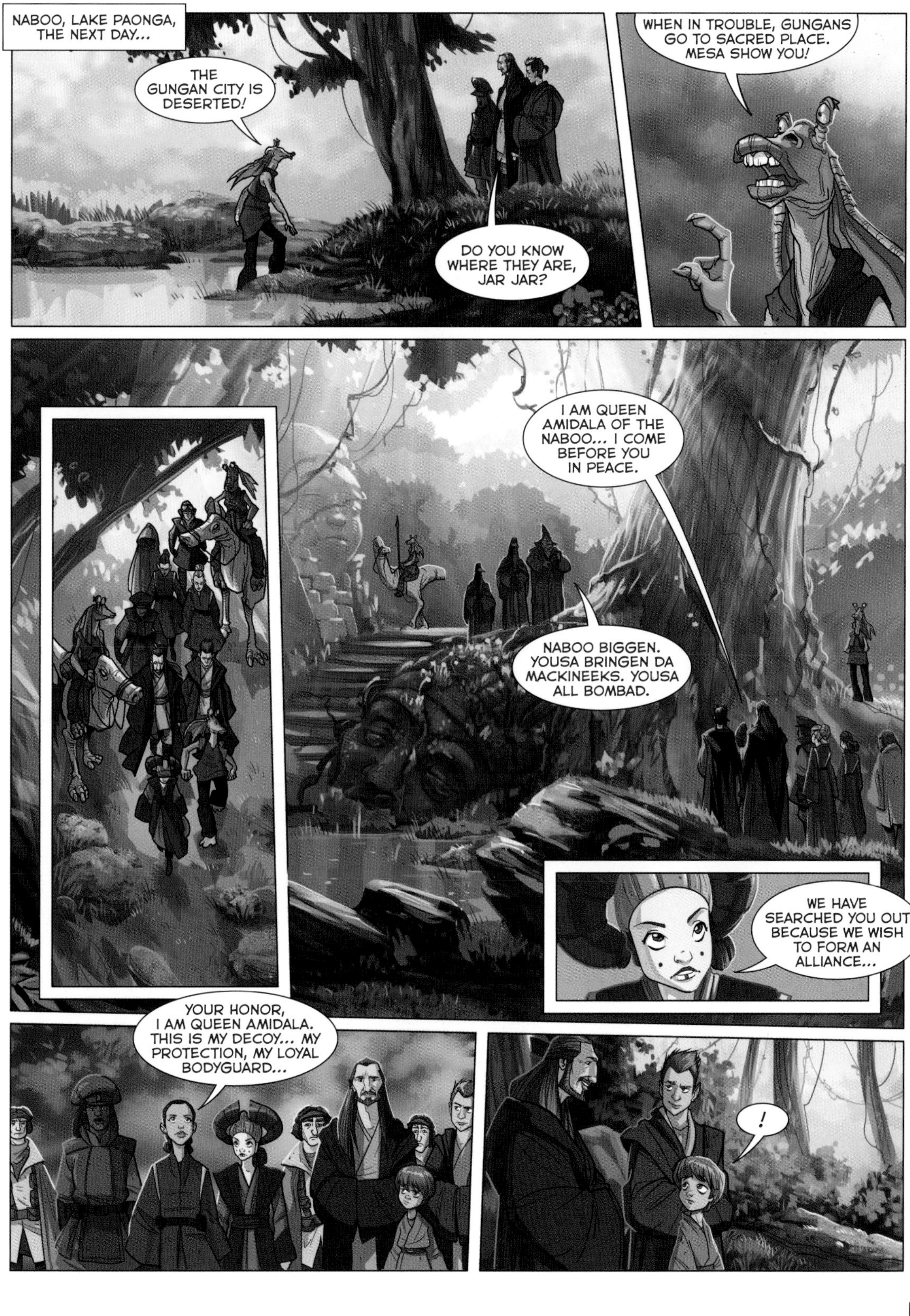

NABOO, LAKE PAONGA, THE NEXT DAY...
THE GUNGAN CITY IS DESERTED!
DO YOU KNOW WHERE THEY ARE, JAR JAR?
WHEN IN TROUBLE, GUNGANS GO TO SACRED PLACE. MESA SHOW YOU!
I AM QUEEN AMIDALA OF THE NABOO... I COME BEFORE YOU IN PEACE.
NABOO BIGGEN. YOUSA BRINGEN DA MACKINEEKS. YOUSA ALL BOMBAD.
WE HAVE SEARCHED YOU OUT BECAUSE WE WISH TO FORM AN ALLIANCE...
YOUR HONOR, I AM QUEEN AMIDALA. THIS IS MY DECOY... MY PROTECTION, MY LOYAL BODYGUARD...
!

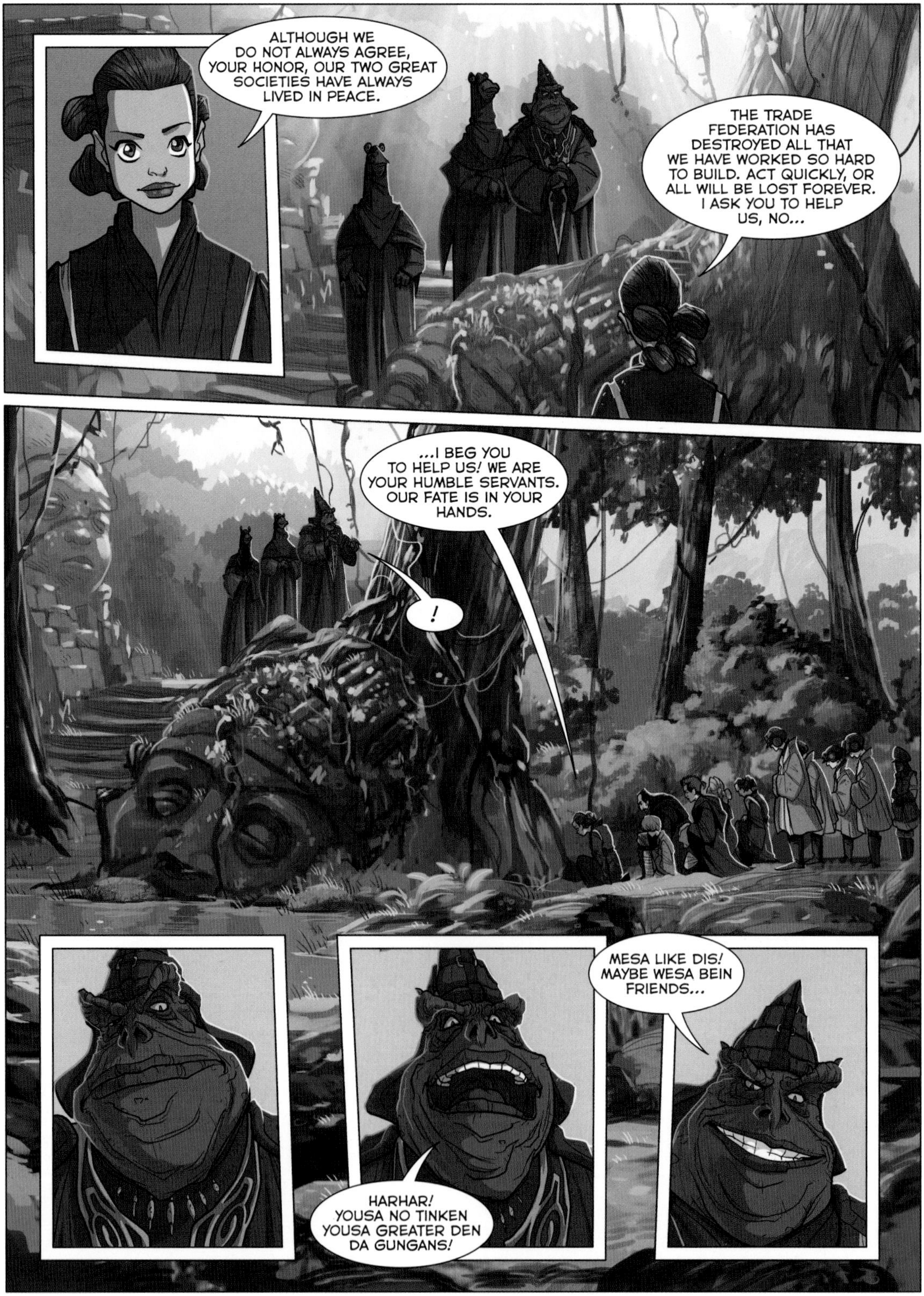
ALTHOUGH WE DO NOT ALWAYS AGREE, YOUR HONOR, OUR TWO GREAT SOCIETIES HAVE ALWAYS LIVED IN PEACE.
THE TRADE FEDERATION HAS DESTROYED ALL THAT WE HAVE WORKED SO HARD TO BUILD. ACT QUICKLY, OR ALL WILL BE LOST FOREVER. I ASK YOU TO HELP US, NO...
...I BEG YOU TO HELP US! WE ARE YOUR HUMBLE SERVANTS. OUR FATE IS IN YOUR HANDS.
!
HARHAR! YOUSA NO TINKEN YOUSA GREATER DEN DA GUNGANS!
MESA LIKE DIS! MAYBE WESA BEIN FRIENDS...

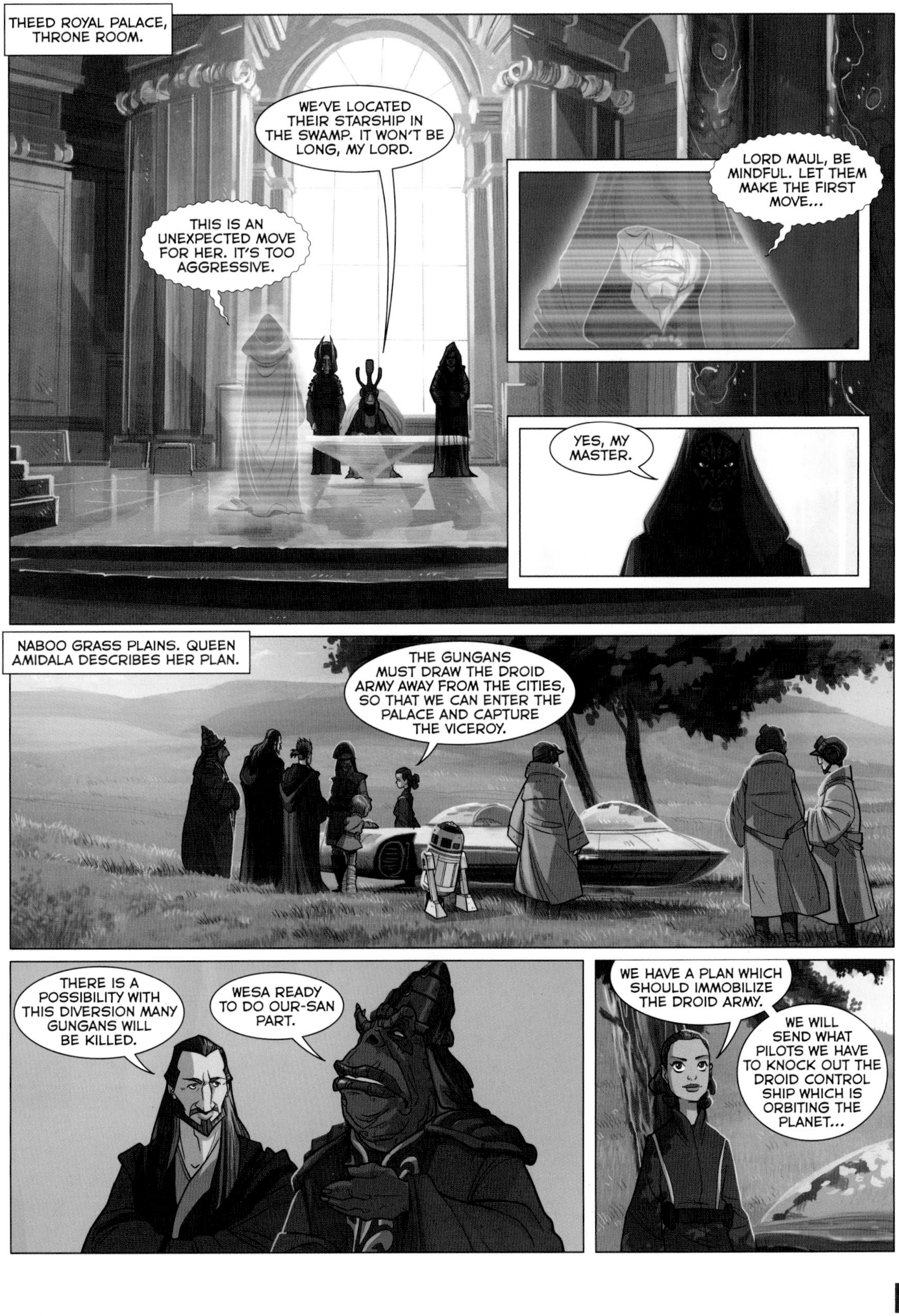
THEED ROYAL PALACE, THRONE ROOM.
WE'VE LOCATED THEIR STARSHIP IN THE SWAMP. IT WON'T BE LONG, MY LORD.
THIS IS AN UNEXPECTED MOVE FOR HER. IT'S TOO AGGRESSIVE.
LORD MAUL, BE MINDFUL. LET THEM MAKE THE FIRST MOVE...
YES, MY MASTER.
NABOO GRASS PLAINS. QUEEN AMIDALA DESCRIBES HER PLAN.
THE GUNGANS MUST DRAW THE DROID ARMY AWAY FROM THE CITIES, SO THAT WE CAN ENTER THE PALACE AND CAPTURE THE VICEROY.
THERE IS A POSSIBILITY WITH THIS DIVERSION MANY GUNGANS WILL BE KILLED.
WESA READY TO DO OUR-SAN PART.
WE HAVE A PLAN WHICH SHOULD IMMOBILIZE THE DROID ARMY.
WE WILL SEND WHAT PILOTS WE HAVE TO KNOCK OUT THE DROID CONTROL SHIP WHICH IS ORBITING THE PLANET...

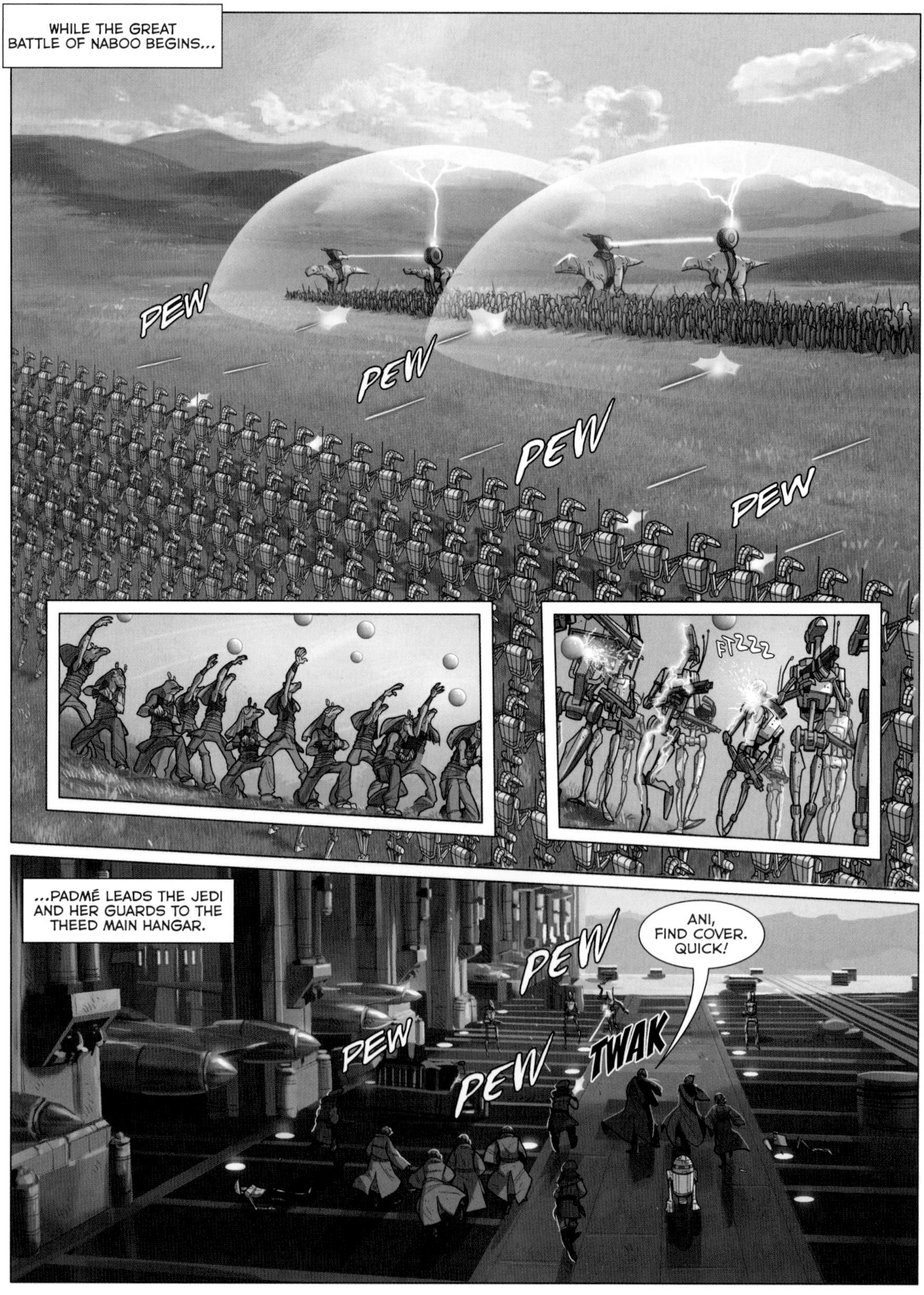
WHILE THE GREAT BATTLE OF NABOO BEGINS...
PEW
PEW
PEW
PEW
FTZZZ
...PADMÉ LEADS THE JEDI AND HER GUARDS TO THE THEED MAIN HANGAR.
PEW
PEW
PEW
TWAK
ANI, FIND COVER. QUICK!

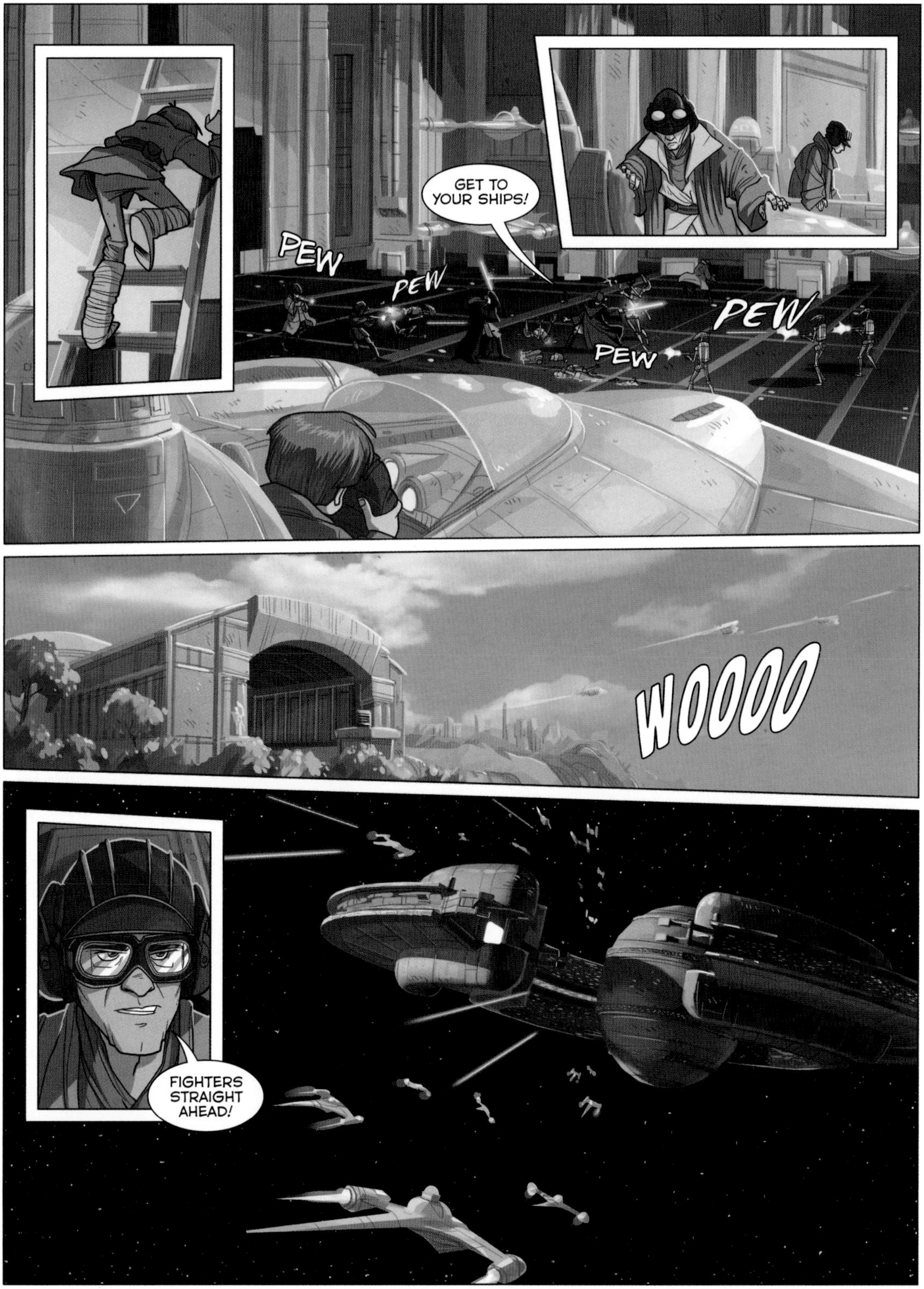

GET TO YOUR SHIPS!
PEW
PEW
PEW
PEW
WOOOO
FIGHTERS STRAIGHT AHEAD!

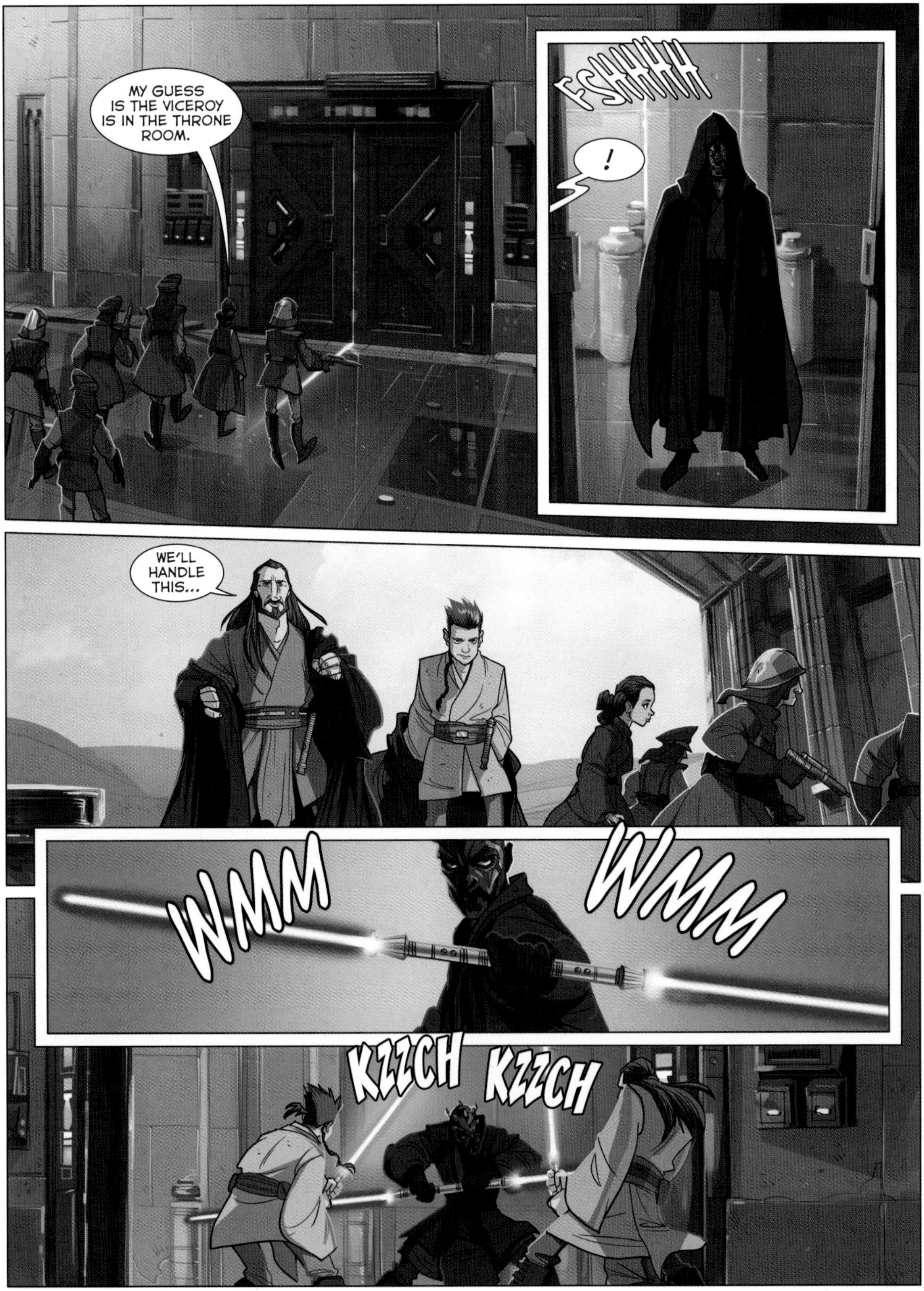
MY GUESS IS THE VICEROY IS IN THE THRONE ROOM.
FCHHHH
!
WE'LL HANDLE THIS...
WMM
WMM
KZZCH
KZZCH

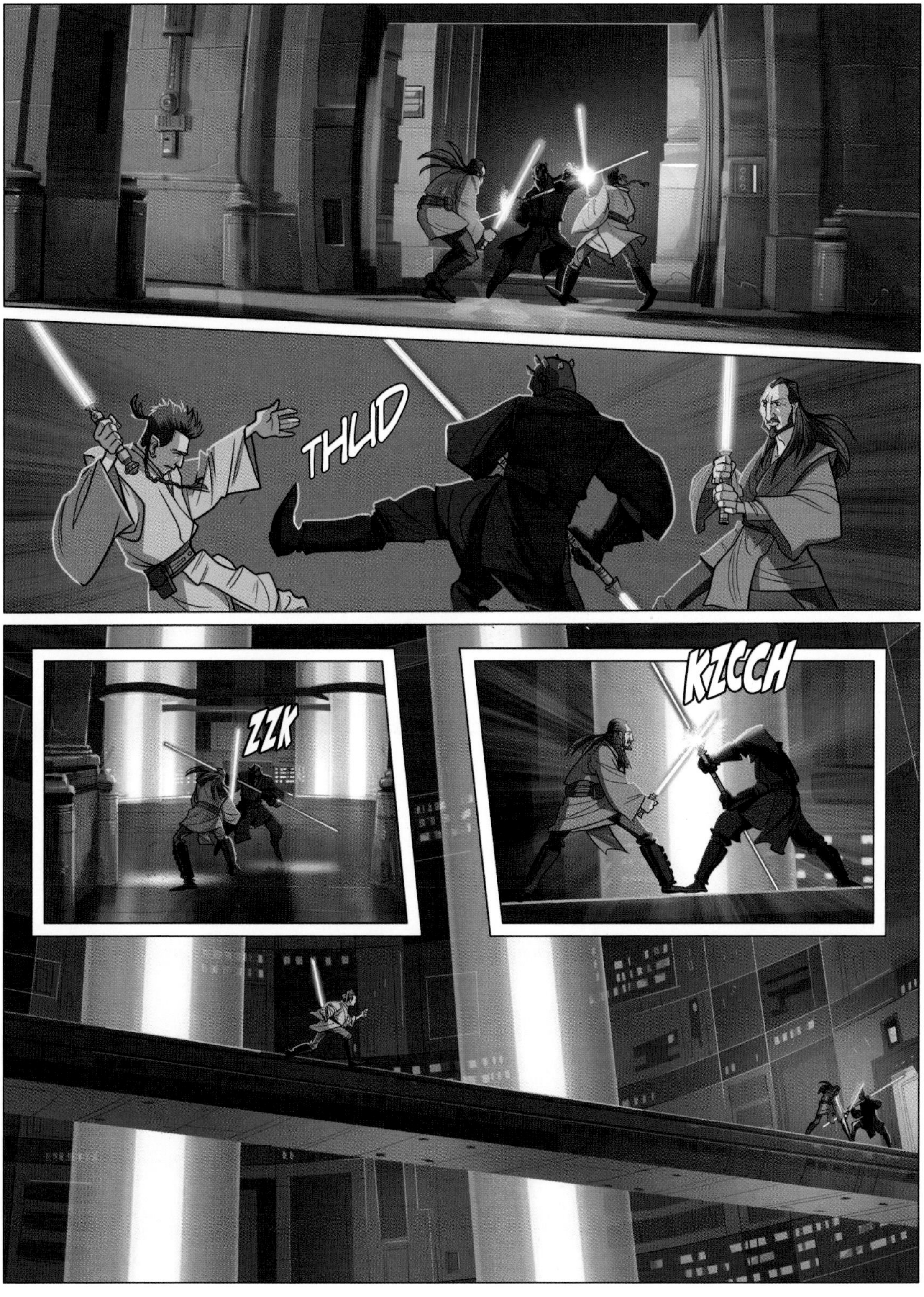
THUD
ZZK
KZCCH

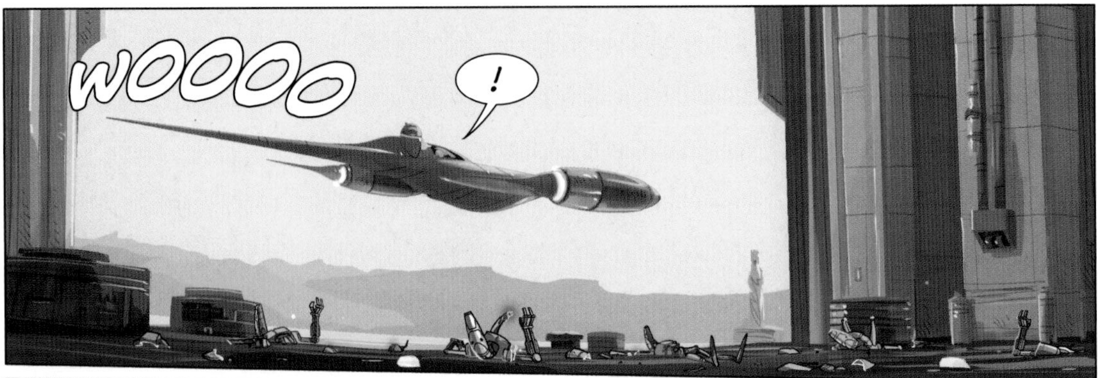
WOOOO
!

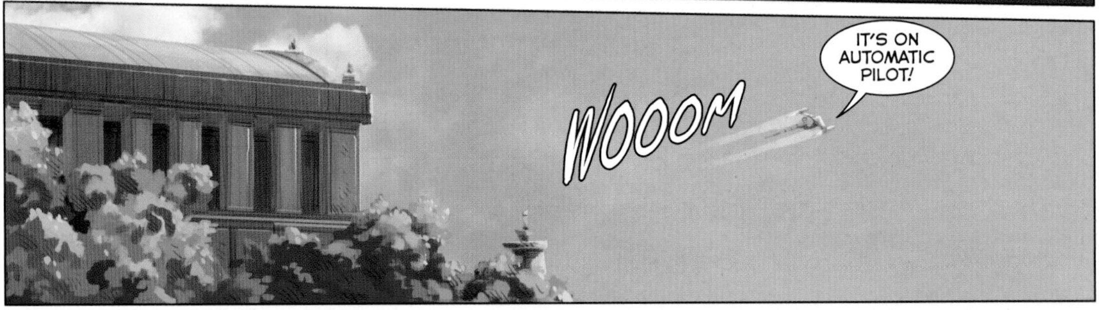
WOOOM
IT'S ON AUTOMATIC PILOT!

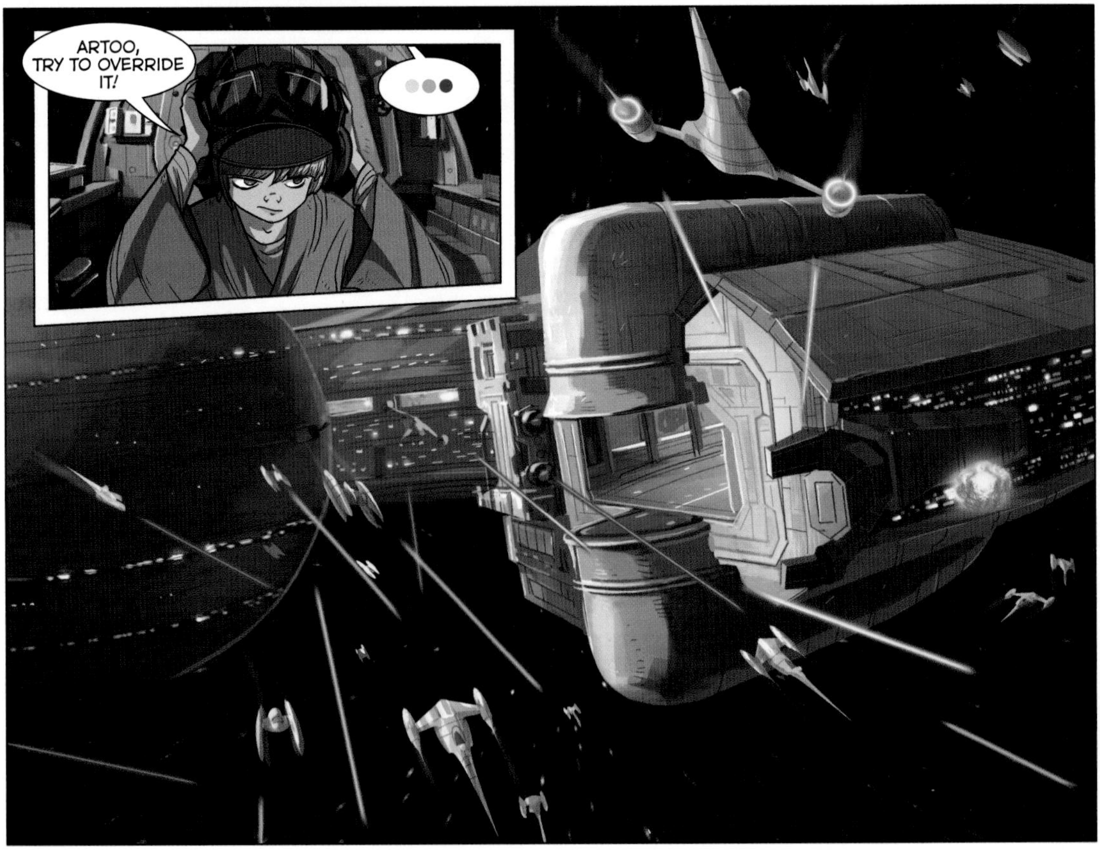
ARTOO, TRY TO OVERRIDE IT!

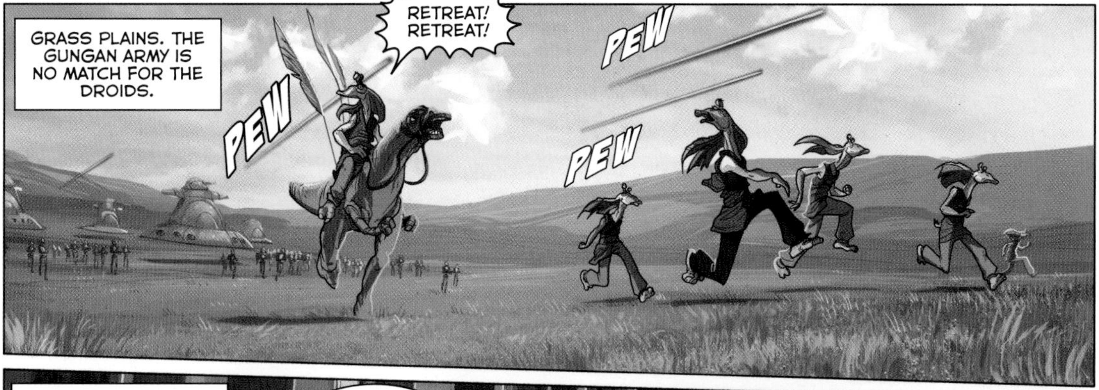
GRASS PLAINS. THE GUNGAN ARMY IS NO MATCH FOR THE DROIDS.
RETREAT! RETREAT!
PEW
PEW
PEW

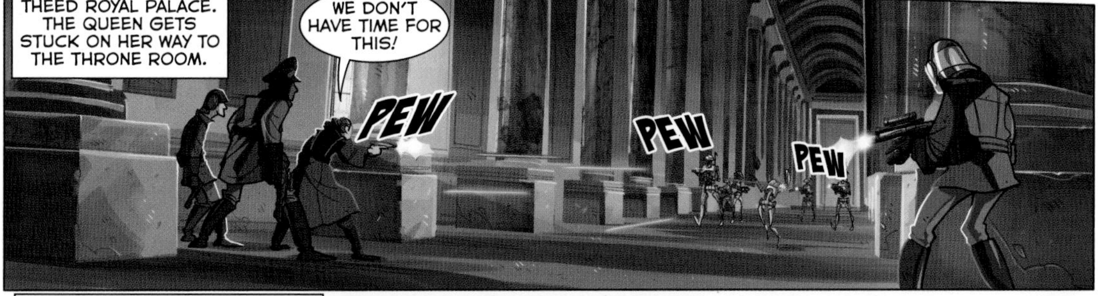
THEED ROYAL PALACE. THE QUEEN GETS STUCK ON HER WAY TO THE THRONE ROOM.
WE DON'T HAVE TIME FOR THIS!
PEW
PEW
PEW

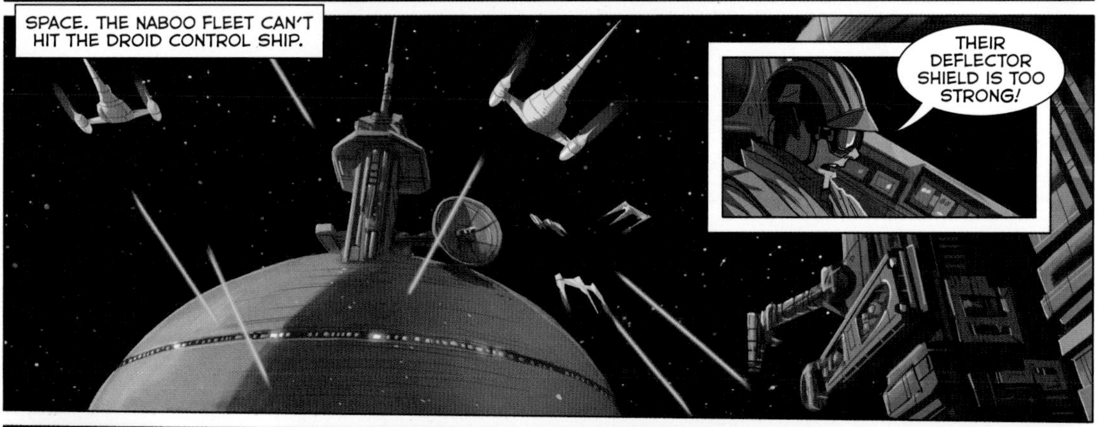
SPACE. THE NABOO FLEET CAN'T HIT THE DROID CONTROL SHIP.
THEIR DEFLECTOR SHIELD IS TOO STRONG!

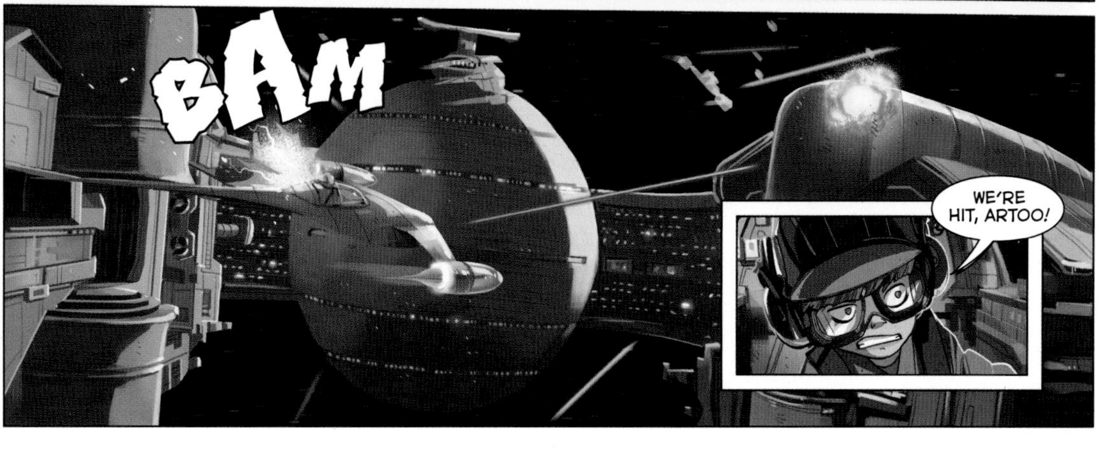
BAM
WE'RE HIT, ARTOO!

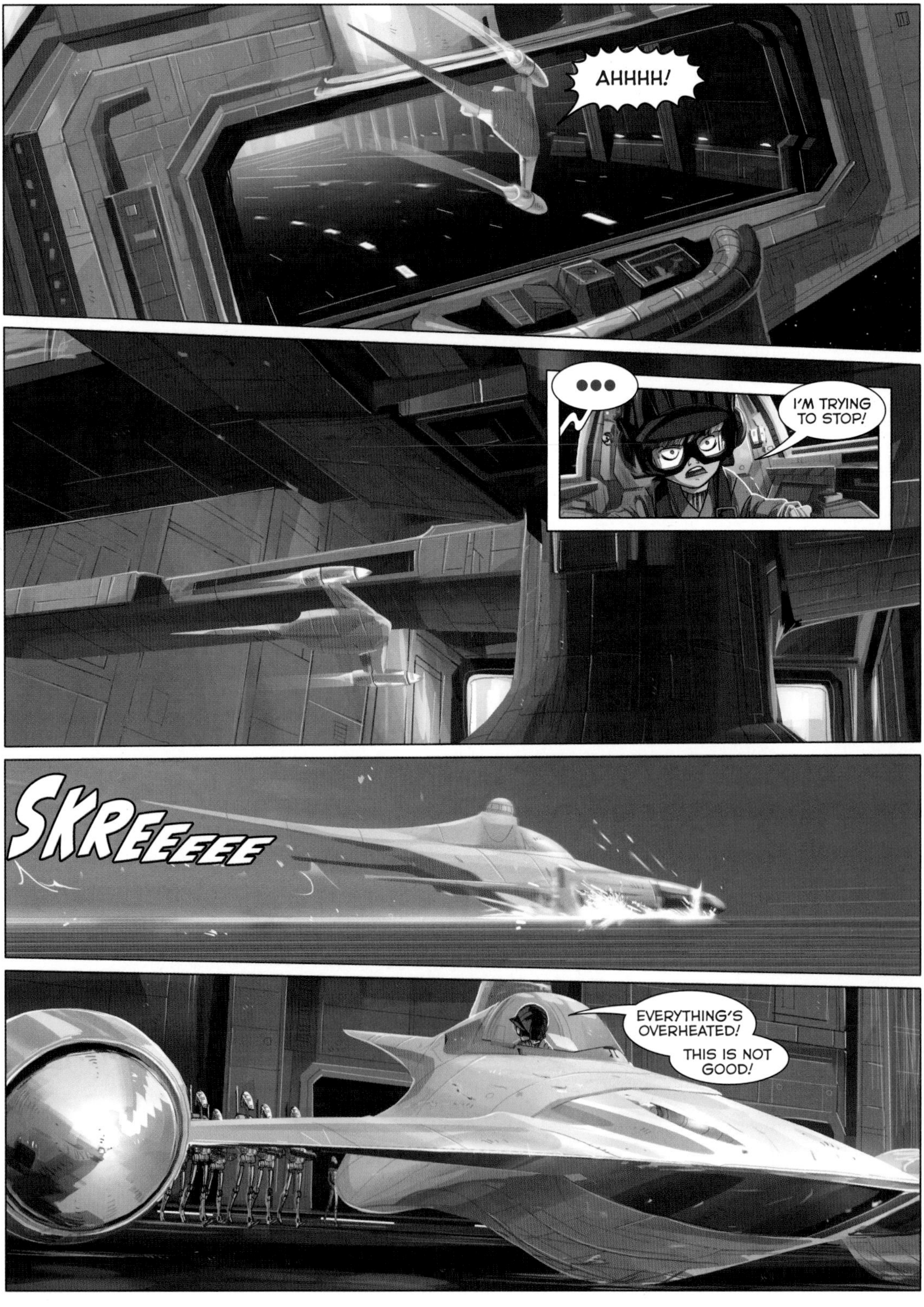
AHHHH!
•••
I'M TRYING TO STOP!
SKREEEEEE
EVERYTHING'S OVERHEATED!
THIS IS NOT GOOD!

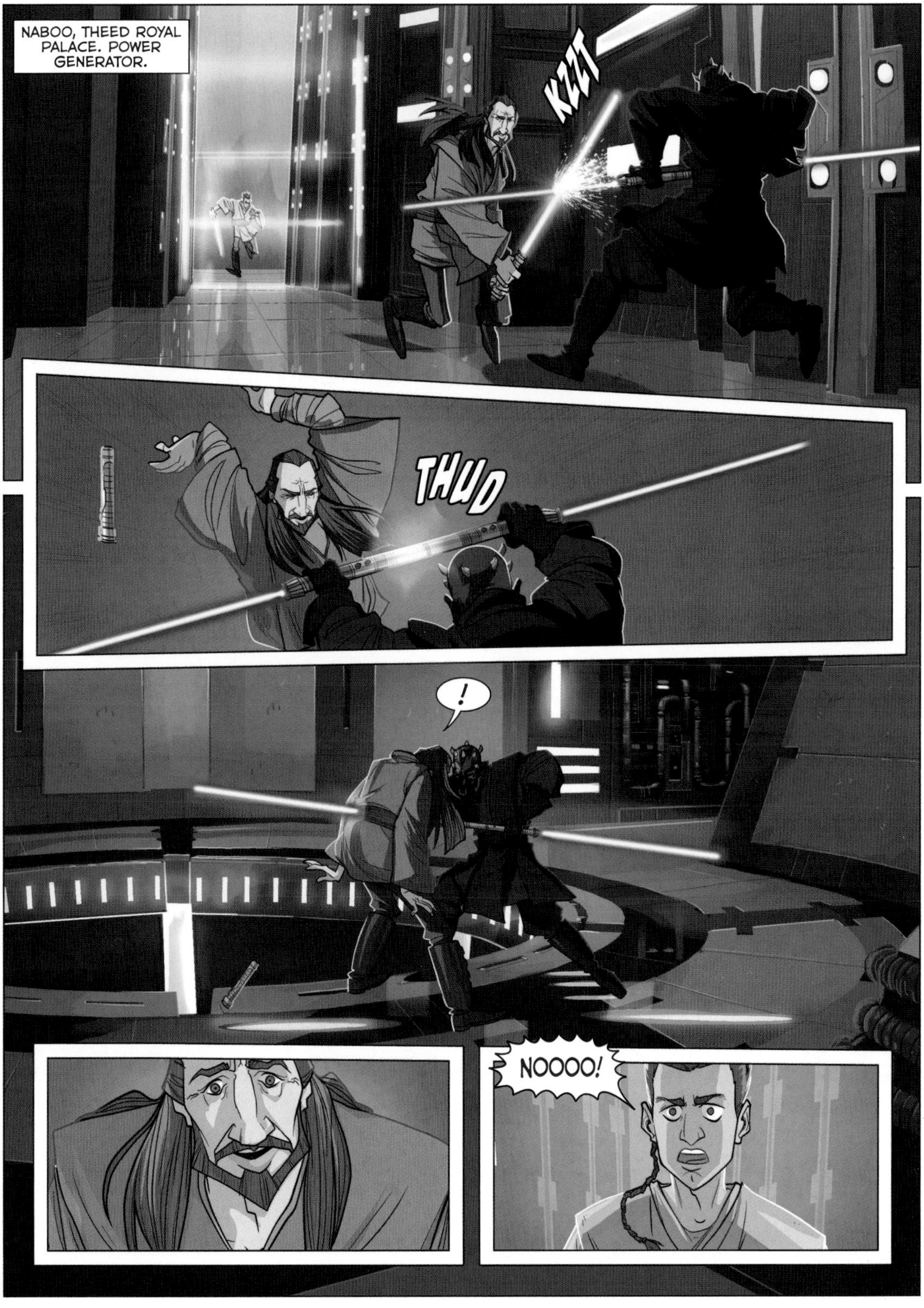

NABOO, THEED ROYAL PALACE. POWER GENERATOR.
KZZT
THUD
!
NOOOO!

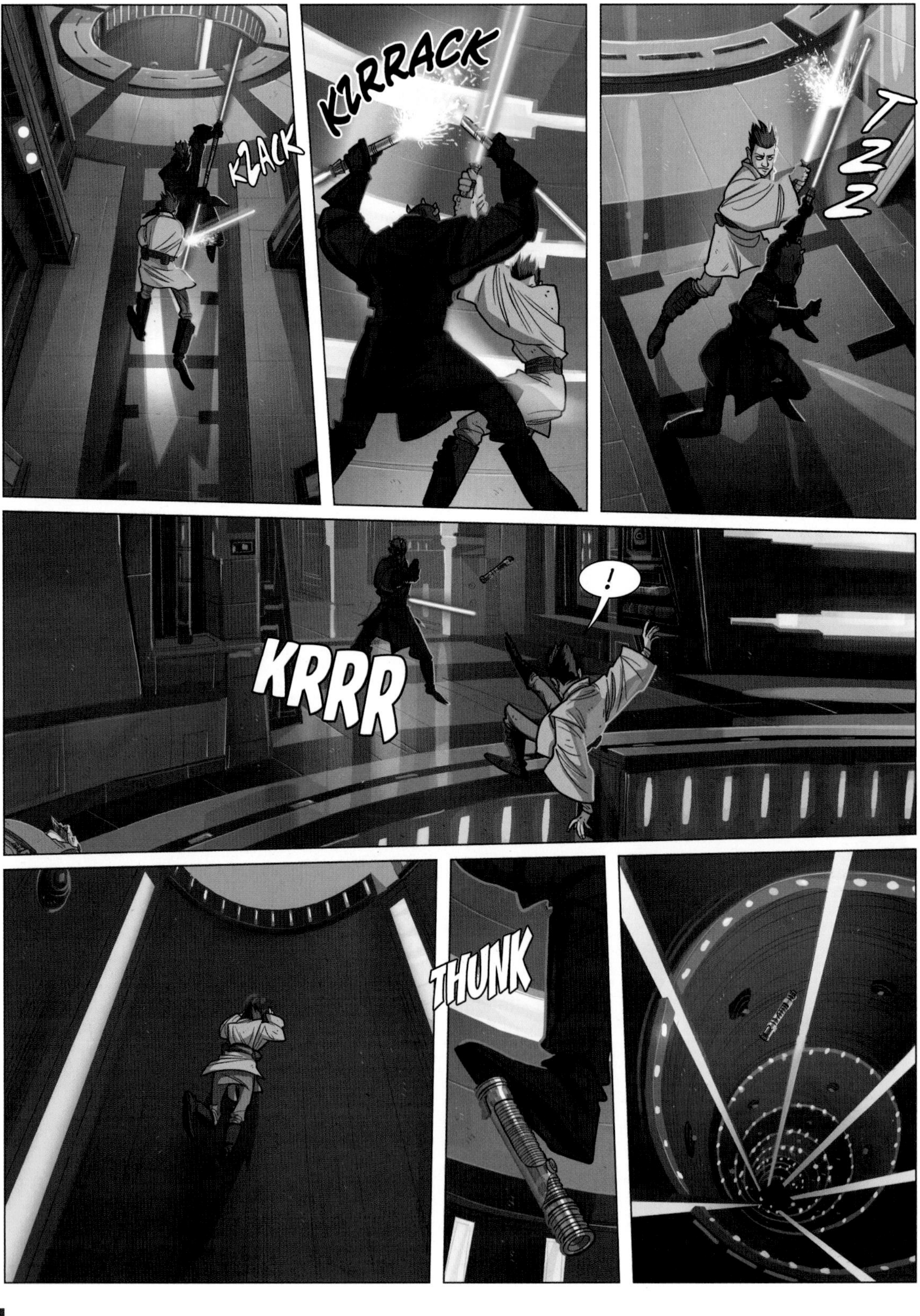
KZACK
KZRRACK
TZZZ
KRRR
!
THUNK

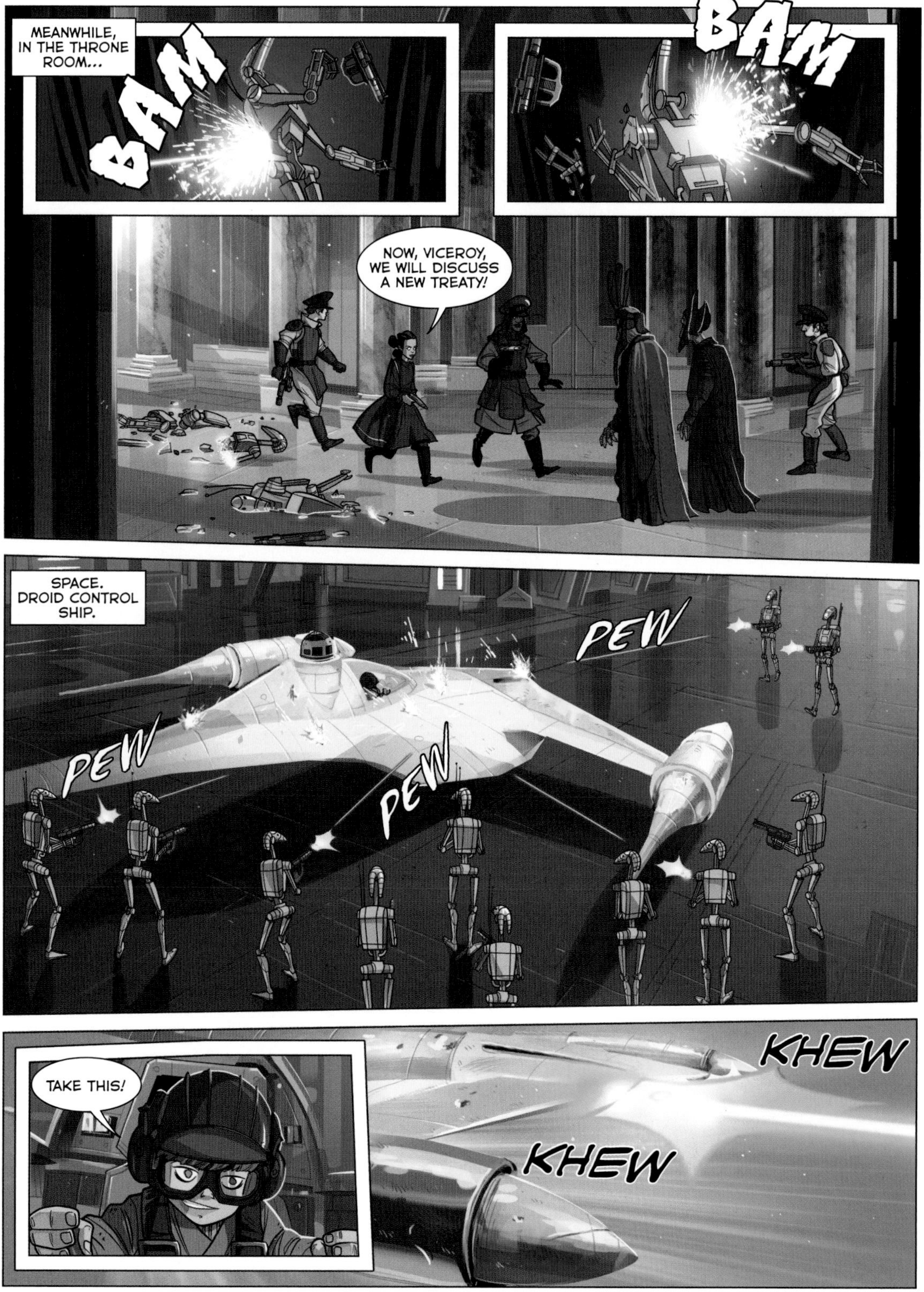
MEANWHILE, IN THE THRONE ROOM...
BAM
BAM
NOW, VICEROY, WE WILL DISCUSS A NEW TREATY!
SPACE. DROID CONTROL SHIP.
PEW
PEW
PEW
TAKE THIS!
KHEW
KHEW

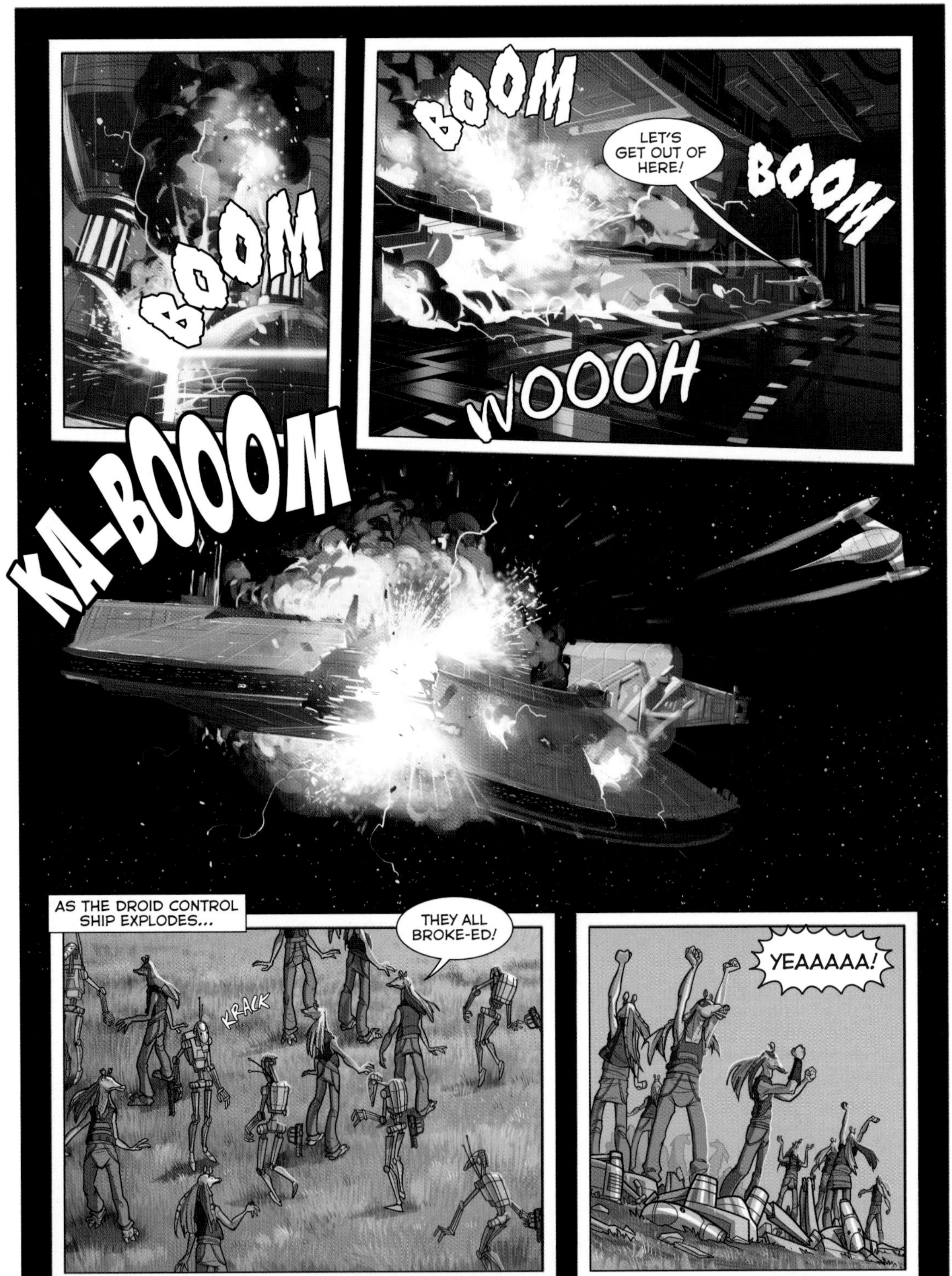
BOOM
BOOM
LET'S GET OUT OF HERE!
BOOM
WOOOH
KA-BOOOM
AS THE DROID CONTROL SHIP EXPLODES...
THEY ALL BROKE-ED!
KRACK
YEAAAAA!

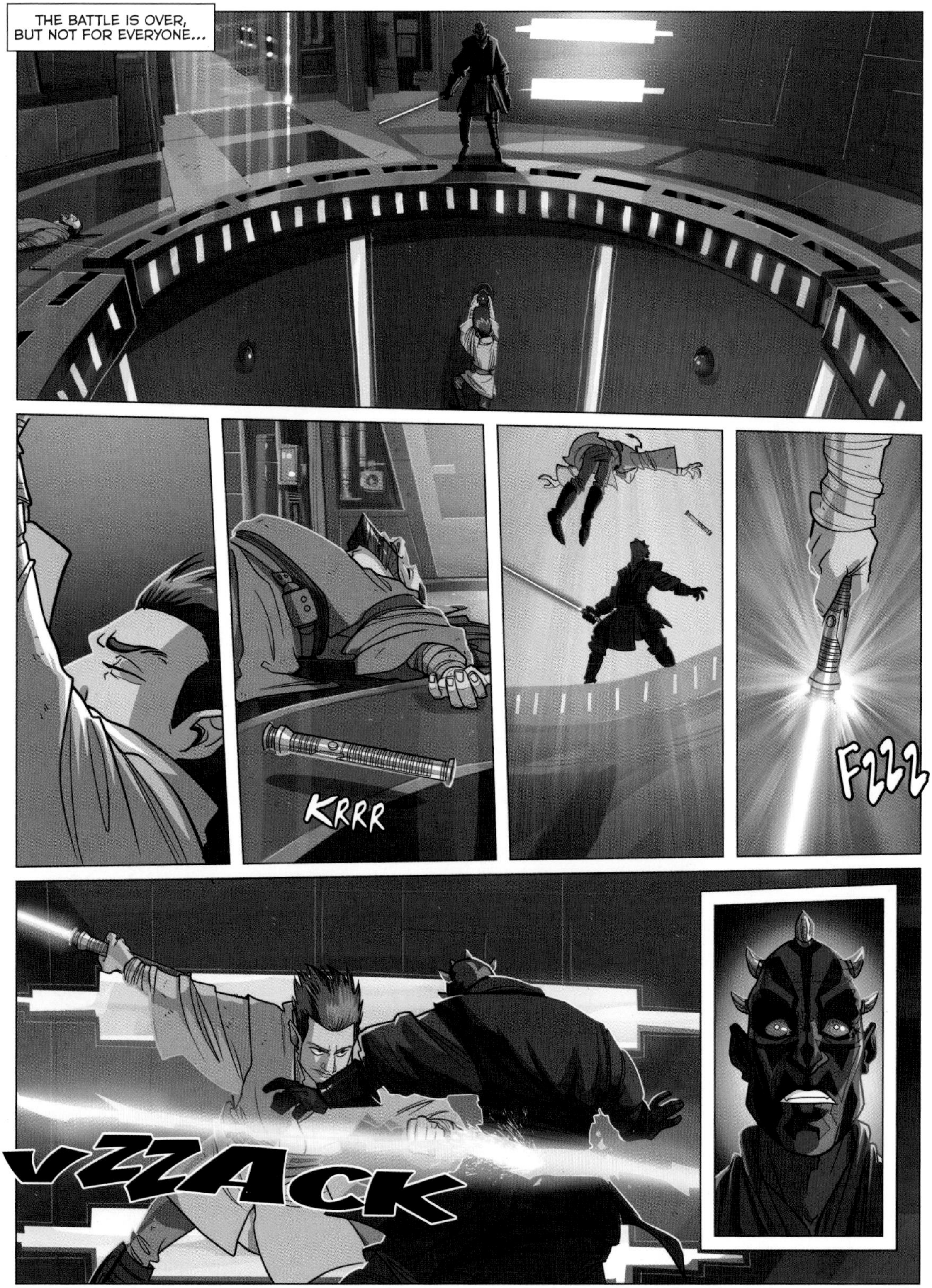
THE BATTLE IS OVER, BUT NOT FOR EVERYONE...
KRRR
FZZZ
VZZACK

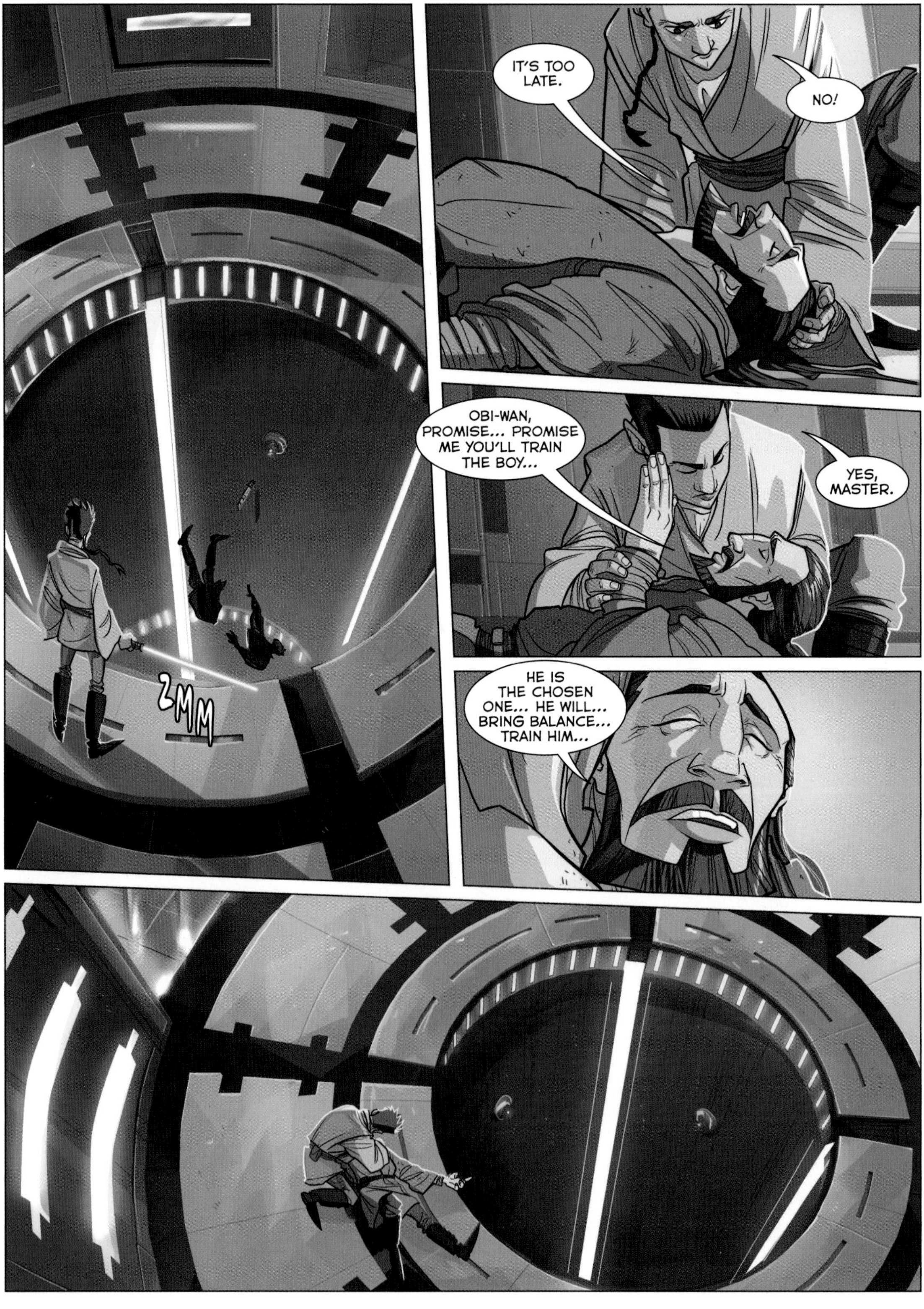
ZMM
IT'S TOO LATE.
NO!
OBI-WAN, PROMISE... PROMISE ME YOU'LL TRAIN THE BOY...
YES, MASTER.
HE IS THE CHOSEN ONE... HE WILL... BRING BALANCE... TRAIN HIM...

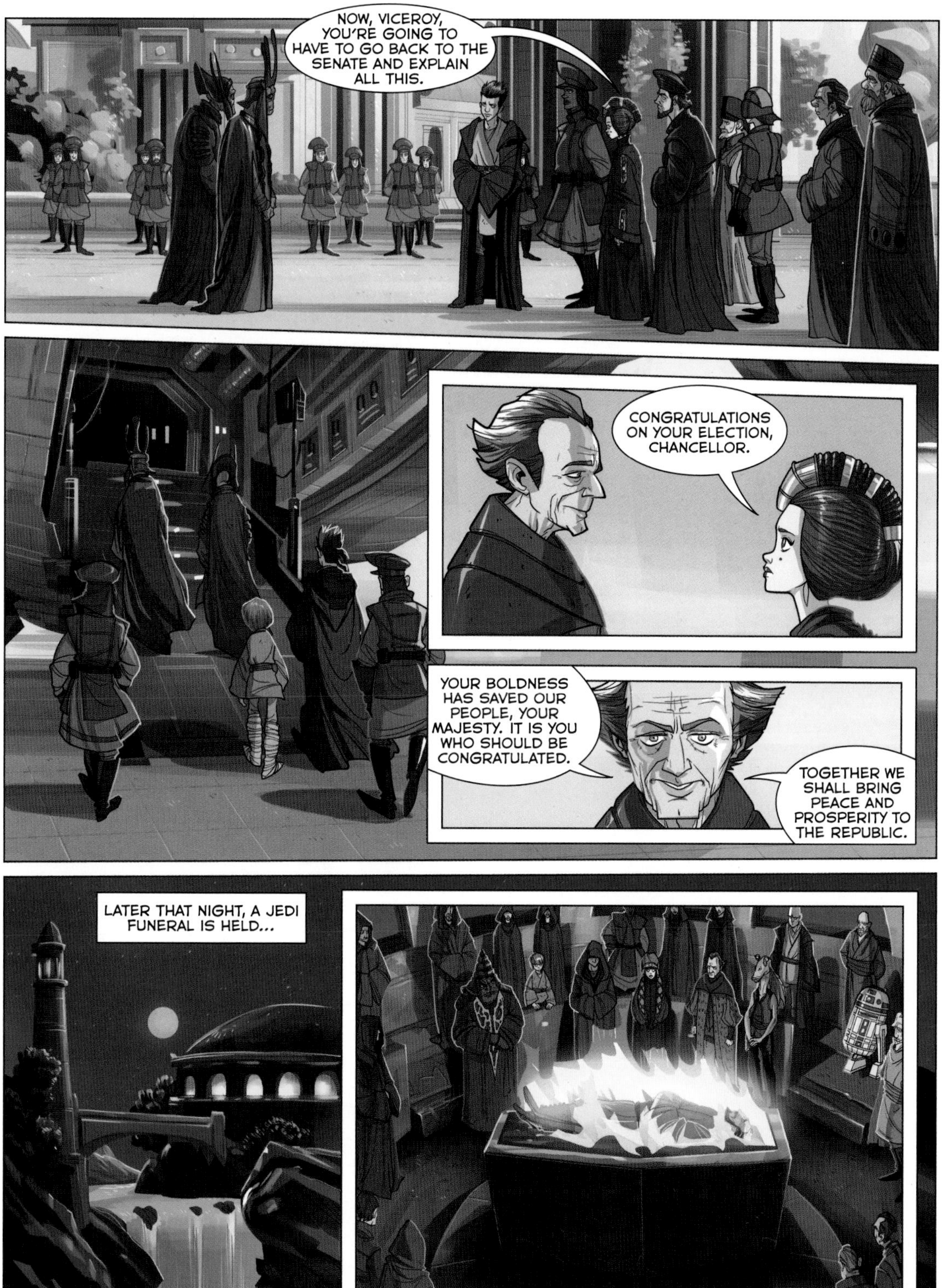
NOW, VICEROY, YOU'RE GOING TO HAVE TO GO BACK TO THE SENATE AND EXPLAIN ALL THIS.
CONGRATULATIONS ON YOUR ELECTION, CHANCELLOR.
YOUR BOLDNESS HAS SAVED OUR PEOPLE, YOUR MAJESTY. IT IS YOU WHO SHOULD BE CONGRATULATED.
TOGETHER WE SHALL BRING PEACE AND PROSPERITY TO THE REPUBLIC.
LATER THAT NIGHT, A JEDI FUNERAL IS HELD...

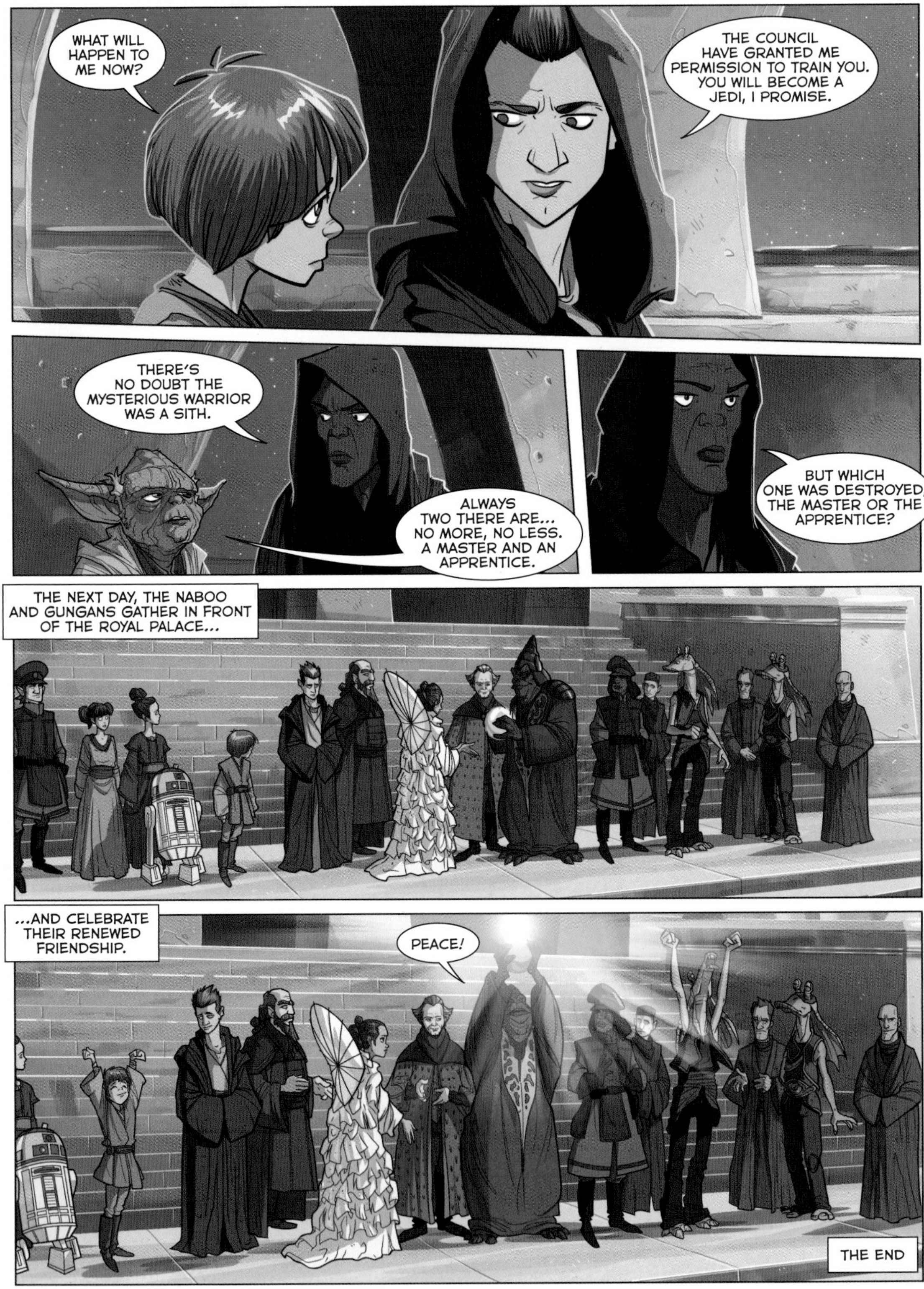
WHAT WILL HAPPEN TO ME NOW?
THE COUNCIL HAVE GRANTED ME PERMISSION TO TRAIN YOU. YOU WILL BECOME A JEDI, I PROMISE.
THERE'S NO DOUBT THE MYSTERIOUS WARRIOR WAS A SITH.
ALWAYS TWO THERE ARE... NO MORE, NO LESS. A MASTER AND AN APPRENTICE.
BUT WHICH ONE WAS DESTROYED, THE MASTER OR THE APPRENTICE?
THE NEXT DAY, THE NABOO AND GUNGANS GATHER IN FRONT OF THE ROYAL PALACE...
...AND CELEBRATE THEIR RENEWED FRIENDSHIP.
PEACE!
THE END

"HE IS THE CHOSEN ONE, YOU MUST SEE IT."

Qui-Gon Jinn

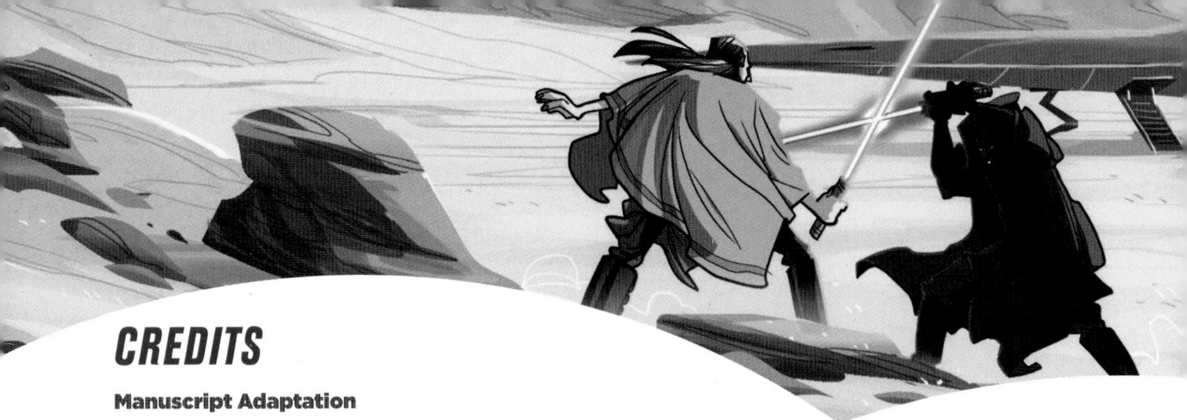

CREDITS

Manuscript Adaptation
Alessandro Ferrari
Character Studies
Igor Chimisso
Layout
Matteo Piana
Clean Up and Ink
Andrea Parisi
Paint (background and settings)
Davide Turotti
Paint (characters)
Kawaii Creative Studio
Cover
Cryssy Cheung
Special Thanks to
Michael Siglain, Jennifer Heddle, Rayne Roberts, Pablo Hidalgo, Leland Chee, Matt Martin

DISNEY PUBLISHING WORLDWIDE
Global Magazines, Comics and Partworks

Editorial Director
Bianca Coletti
Editorial Team
Guido Frazzini *(Director, Comics)*
Stefano Ambrosio *(Executive Editor, New IP)*
Carlotta Quattrocolo *(Executive Editor, Franchise)*
Camilla Vedove *(Senior Manager, Editorial Development)*
Behnoosh Khalili *(Senior Editor)*
Julie Dorris *(Senior Editor)*
Design
Enrico Soave *(Senior Designer)*

Art
Ken Shue *(VP, Global Art)*
Roberto Santillo *(Creative Director)*
Marco Ghiglione *(Creative Manager)*
Stefano Attardi *(Illustration Manager)*
Portfolio Management
Olivia Ciancarelli *(Director)*
Business & Marketing
Mariantonietta Galla *(Marketing Manager)*, Virpi Korhonen *(Editorial Manager)*, Kristen Ginter *(Publishing Coordinator)*
Editing – Graphic Design
Absink, Edizioni BD
Contributors
Carlo Resca

For IDW:
Editors:
Alonzo Simon and Zac Boone

Collection Design:
Clyde Grapa

Lucasfilm Credits:
Robert Simpson, Senior Editor
Michael Siglain, Creative Director
Phil Szostak, Lucasfilm Art Department
Matt Martin, Pablo Hidalgo, and Emily Shkoukani, Story Group

Based on the story by George Lucas

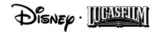

For international rights, contact **licensing@idwpublishing.com**

ISBN: 978-1-68405-638-5

24 23 22 21 1 2 3 4

Nachie Marsham, Publisher • **Rebekah Cahalin**, EVP of Operations • **Blake Kobashigawa**, VP of Sales • **John Barber**, Editor-in-Chief • **Justin Eisinger**, Editorial Director, Graphic Novels & Collections • **Scott Dunbier**, Director, Special Projects • **Anna Morrow**, Sr Marketing Director **Tara McCrillis**, Director of Design & Production • **Shauna Monteforte**, Manufacturing Operations Director

Ted Adams and Robbie Robbins, IDW Founders

www.IDWPUBLISHING.com

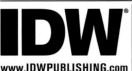

Facebook: **facebook.com/idwpublishing** • Twitter: **@idwpublishing**
YouTube: **youtube.com/idwpublishing** • Instagram: **@idwpublishing**

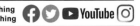